and yet they were happy

helen phillips

A LeapLit Book
Leapfrog Literature
Leapfrog Press
Teaticket, Massachusetts

A LeapLit Book
Leapfrog Literature

Published in 2011 in the United States by
Leapfrog Press LLC
PO Box 2110
Teaticket, MA 02536
www.leapfrogpress.com

Distributed in the United States by
Consortium Book Sales and Distribution
St. Paul, Minnesota 55114
www.cbsd.com

Printed in the United States

First Edition

Library of Congress Cataloging-in-Publication Data

Phillips, Helen, 1983-
  And yet they were happy / Helen Phillips. -- 1st ed.
     p. cm.
  ISBN 978-1-935248-18-7 (alk. paper)
  I. Title.
  PS3616.H45565A83 2011
  813'.6--dc22
     2011003402

for my parents
and
for Adam

contents

the floods

flood #1

The old family farm is going to drown. They've built a dam downriver. The cow-dung meadow will be flooded, the disintegrating tractor and the dandelions. You can't think of anything to do but throw an enormous party.

Your parents. Your sisters. Your brother. Your grandparents. Your step-grandmother. Your aunts, uncles, cousins; the greats and the seconds, the in-laws and the friends. The guy you once screamed at in the street. The person who shrieked at you in the zoo. The woman who got secretly divorced; the woman who got secretly married. The people who keep dead songbirds in their freezer. The old lady who prepares faces for burial. The couple on the L.L. Bean catalogue. Arctic brides, amateur astronomers, nine pirates, 112 magicians. All the wedding guests, and all the Helen Phillipses. The beekeeper flirting with the blind woman, Persephone flirting with the fatigued photographer, Bob Dylan grudgingly whirling the girl who thought she was a mermaid, Jack Kerouac making big promises to the Neanderthals, Anne Frank slow-dancing with St. Nick, Snow White on a hay bale braiding Mary's hair, Eve chasing your unborn daughter, the man at table 14 trying to amuse glum Noah, Charlie Chaplin aping Adam, the detectives goading the firemen, Orpheus telling the alien the violinist can't fiddle to save his life. Not to mention the things emerging from the dark of the woods: beast, unicorn, monster, dragon, animals lined up two by two.

Everyone! That's all you want. Everyone!

You just want everyone to be there, drinking beer, drinking cheap red wine, eating cakes and cookies, lingering by the bonfire, you want to look up at the soft black sky with its mournful stars and then look down to see everyone standing around the bonfire, starting to dance around the bonfire, jubilant, guitar and banjo, harmonica and tambourine, trying to have the time of our lives as the river begins to rise, water coming like snakes through the tall grasses and the blackberry brambles, lifting plastic cups and paper napkins, the river rising, rising.

flood #2

Tonight an old man came in and asked for honey mead. That's not a request we get much nowadays, and I kept a close eye on him. His beard was outrageously long. I couldn't see the end of it from where I stood behind the bar. It had things, twigs and leaves, stuck so far into it that I wondered if they hadn't been intentionally woven among the strands. His hair too was chaotic. A bird could've built a nice home there. Walt Whitman times a hundred, I thought to myself.

This old man was not like our other patrons. He didn't glance in the direction of the pool tables, and he was oblivious to even our prettiest girl. With each cup of honey mead, he crumpled further into himself. Eventually I noticed that his beard was soggy. I leaned over the bar in a manner that has been known to make old guys tell their stories.

"I didn't get them all," he said.

"What all?"

"Madam." He looked at me for the first time. His

eyes were golden, no kidding. "There were small elephants. Beautiful little elephants no larger than housecats." I nodded. "Madam, there were mice the size of rhinos and rhinos the size of this building. Fire-breathing iguanas with gentle dispositions. Six-eyed crocodiles that spouted like whales. Squirrels as ferocious as lions. Turtles with opposable thumbs. Miniature foxes living in treetop nests. Cranes as big as cranes. Dragonflies that flew faster than your airplanes. Doves that flew backward. Blue giraffes. Vegetarian tigers. Bloodthirsty mountain sheep. Antelope with wings."

I stroked his wobbling hand. His beard was getting downright wet. I hung on to his finger. I've seen a lot of sad crazy old men. But this guy, he was different. He was not crazy, and he had every reason in this godforsaken universe to be sad.

"The rain kept coming," he said. "It became difficult to gather them two by two." I was stricken by the length and filth of his nails. "At times," he said, "impossible."

flood #3

On a planet other than our own, Eve and Noah stroll through an apple orchard at sundown. Swallows dip and whirr above them. The honeybees have vanished for the night. Soon the bats will come out. The grass is wet from an afternoon storm. Above, the sky darkens from light blue to blue. It is impossible to avoid stepping on and crushing clover blossoms. Eve reaches for Noah's hand. They have lived on this farm for many centuries. They are very old, but tonight they don't feel so old.

Once, long ago, when Eve was a young wife, she ate a gleaming apple off a tree in this very orchard; and nothing happened. And Noah, when he was a young husband, became convinced that a large wooden boat ought to be built. Every night he had these dreams, and every morning he recited to Eve a litany of horrors: enormous oaks struck by lightning, a rainstorm that lasted forty days, the death of every single creature they didn't personally rescue, a lone mountaintop poking above the water, the barren mud flats where their farm had been, monstrous solitude. Eve, a good and patient wife, helped him, holding nails in her mouth while he hammered.

The half-built ark still sits there behind the cottage. Honeysuckle, wild ivy, and squash vines have grown up and over it. Partway through the construction of the ark, their daughter was born; the nightmares ceased; and Noah turned his attention to coaxing things out of the soil, which was suffering from a lack of water rather than an excess of it. Eve sighed with relief, baked a batch of her bitter almond cake, kept her daughter strapped to her all day because her breasts produced an ungodly amount of milk, and grinned privately when she noticed tendrils creeping over the abandoned boat. Sometimes, on nights such as this, when they lie in bed with their skeletal limbs entwined, Eve mocks Noah for his youthful belief in nightmares, in obedience, in orders from someone other than her.

flood #4

So often that spring, my parents were worried. They woke early and looked at the falling rain. It rained and rained. The days were warm and wet. It was the kind of weather that makes worms and crocuses rise. Mom groaned. Dad kept saying, "The basement better not flood, then we'd have a goddamn problem on our hands." I almost laughed whenever Dad said goddamn.

"How deep will the water be?" I said.

"That's not the way it works," Mom said. "It seeps, that's how it works."

"It's not going to be deep and it's not going to seep," Dad said, "because it's not going to flood at all."

"Deep and seep!" I said. "That rhymes. You're a poet and you didn't even know it."

But my parents weren't listening. They were looking at the rain.

A flooded house! It sounded wonderful, like a swimming pool; I pictured myself swimming around, gazing at all the familiar objects preserved and undisturbed in the blue chlorinated clarity.

I wanted the house to flood oh how I wanted it to flood!

I'd use my nascent swimming skills to propel myself into the kitchen. I'd look at the table beneath me: half a grapefruit and a toothed spoon. Mom's food. In the living room, I'd float past the underwater books, Dad's old leather books, stroking them with my tiptoes. The bathroom would be funny, the toilet far below, its water joined to the floodwater, and the bathtub submerged. In my bedroom, the dolls would be transformed into mermaids; they'd stare up at me, a green cast to their hair. Perhaps the sun would break through, glowing in the window, and I'd do a water somersault. Next my parents' bedroom, the large maroon pillows still puffy as ever, and then the guestroom, which was now my dad's bedroom.

The basement did flood, and that made the septic system flood, and there was old poop all over the carpet, and my parents had to clean it up, and they were not happy, not happy at all.

flood #5

The floodwaters are rising. First, we notice starfish in the subway (initially mistaken for the handprints of homeless men smeared on the tile); we notice sea cucumbers on the tracks (initially mistaken for the discarded produce of tired old Russian ladies). We are charmed by the appearance of these oceanic creatures (indeed, we give them credit for their gumption, to end up here) until we realize what their appearance reveals. . . . And in the park we come upon a lone white duck with wild, filthy feathers; he marches along the shore of the lake, waiting for the water to come to him. This duck—he scares us. He's a brave crazy fellow, and delighted that the floodwaters are rising; he'd kill us if he could. A handful of tiny birds takes flight from a chokecherry bush. It is impossible to decipher their feelings about the floodwaters. They are so stupid and beautiful, always following one another in perfect formation, moving up and down in the air like black pearls strung on an invisible net.

      Oh—darling—watch those metaphors, you're getting ornate, you're starting to use metaphors from the sea, do you even know what a black pearl is, because I don't. You wouldn't be talking about black pearls if you didn't know, somewhere deep inside, that the floodwaters truly are rising.

We go to the grocery store, where we *These fragments I have shored* don't know what to buy we try *These fragments I have shored against* to think logically but fail so we *These fragments I have shored against my* grab tofu Oreos cinnamon bananas birthday *These fragments I have shored against my ruins* candles chicken who keeps saying that anyway someone keeps saying something I keep hearing it—

Please—darling—you've got to focus, and stay calm. The floodwaters are rising. Didn't you see the tree that got struck by lightning? Didn't you see how the top fell to the bottom, and how all the leaves and red berries that were once out of reach are now on the ground?

flood #6

They tell us our apples have poisonous skin. We smile, thinking of Snow White, most beloved fairytale. But they're dead serious. They send lists out to the newspapers: *Apples, Carrots, Grapes, Lettuce, Peaches, Peppers, Potatoes, Tomatoes.* Virtually the only produce to which we have access, and all poisonous! We're warned that our babies will be born blind, or two-headed. Clutching our abdomens, we attempt to reassure one another. Tea? someone proposes, and we nod, until we discover an article about the dangers of tap water. When boiled, it unleashes substances that cause babies to be born without fingers. We sit in the kitchen, neither drinking tea nor eating apples. Sitting there bored, frightened, we'd take comfort in breathing deeply, but already our lungs are dangerously black. *Your chromosomes will crack. You'll lose the ability to hold a fetus.* Breathing shallow, as we've been trained, we look out the window and pity the air. Once upon a time, that air was as clean as it looks! It entered joyous lungs. It powered great feats of athleticism and song. At sunset, it was reminiscent of honey. Nowadays the sky gets red and purple. The sunsets of our era are grander than the sunsets of any other. Our ragged air does something miraculous and terrifying to light. We recall the tips for tranquility our mothers offered us before we abandoned them. *Eat apples. Drink tea. Breathe deeply. Go to the park.* Our dear idiotic mothers! In the park, garbage blows like snow and a plastic bag frozen into the lake looks like a duck trapped under ice. *Take care of yourself,* our mothers said. We go to the pharmacy to pick up our necessary prescriptions, the prescriptions that will keep us normal and secure, but we mistrust the pharmacists. What if we threw these prescriptions into the overflowing puddles beneath the bus? What if we buried them in the soggy park? We hear of babies born with traces of twenty-seven poisons in their umbilical cords. We sit in the kitchen, eating nothing.

we?

we? #1

Man and Woman, very old, stooped over, waiting at crosswalk.

Meanwhile, we're discontent with the bodies of our youth. Our legs seem too short, our spines insufficiently elongated, our stomachs flabby. We don't live in a swoon of desire. We're no Adam and Eve. We don't chase each other nakedly, ecstatically, around the bedroom. Yours cannot be compared to a tree, nor mine to a flower. We don't wake desirous in the night. No matter how much we scrub, our feet stink. Our breath smells inexplicably of cheese. We've seen a rock-star with the nose of a king; we've seen a girl on the bus with the lips of a queen. But we are not they. Several white hairs have already emerged. Thousands of meals lie ahead of us; someone will have to clean the kitchen each time.

Eventually, it will become a practical matter, millions of yours searching for one of mine. A little beast will develop between us. When it's born it will be a skinny, flexible thing with untouched skin. Our hearts will explode, expand. Wearily, we'll embrace, and someday soon, we'll be old.

Forgive me. A revision:

Meanwhile, we're grateful for the bodies of our youth. Our legs are strong, our vertebrae stacked like a row of faithful turtles, our stomachs covered with a layer of fat like mammals preparing for hibernation. Beneath our blanket, we cling to each other. We're Adam and Eve living through the first winter on Earth. When one of us stumbles naked to the toilet, the other is left behind, getting cold, listening to the sound of pee. When the pee-er returns, the bed becomes warm again, and words are exchanged. Spend enough time around a bad smell, and you no longer smell it. Kings and queens are unwelcome here. I count your white hairs like a kid counting starfish.

The light changes. Man and Woman begin to cross the street. They're so stooped over it looks as though they're searching for things on the pavement: pennies, lost tickets, apple seeds.

we? #2

In the park, everyone is dehydrated. Like shipwrecked sailors who've finally reached land, everyone sprawls pathetically on the grass. Babies born in winter learn, for the first time, of sun. Skinny girls and fat girls pull up their skirts, revealing everything. Grass sticks to their thighs. The sky blue shirts of the college boys are soaked with Frisbee sweat. A teenager sits under a tree, struggles with his guitar, bestows upon everyone mismatched chords, a king throwing coins to the poor. Everyone is sunburned. A young man and a young woman lie side by side on the grass. Her heart swells, swells, shrinks, shrinks, swells, swells, shrinks, shrinks. Unaware of this turmoil, his heart plods patiently. *Your joy—it shall be unbounded.* Swelling, swelling, shrinking, shrinking. Are there a million people here? Nowhere near a million, you're so bad with numbers. Fine, then, are there two hundred? Way more than two hundred. Fine, then, Mr. Perfect, how many people? *Your joy—it shall be unbounded.* Today, someone has turned twenty-five. So young, yet now this person's age can be easily measured in terms of centuries. Old people find shaded benches, wishing to avoid dehydration and sunburn. But when you're young, being dehydrated and sunburned resembles being drunk. *Your joy*— Shrinking, shrinking, swelling, swelling. That child over there has absolutely no fine motor skills! Look! Whenever he tries to throw the ball it slips right out of his hands. We'll have children. Won't we? —*it shall be unbounded*. Are you thirsty? I said, are you thirsty? No. *Your*— You're thirsty, I can tell, I can see it in your eyes. I'm not thirsty. Shrinking, shrinking. You are thirsty. *It shall be unbounded*. That baby's mother has a huge ass. I hope I never have an ass like that. She has a nice face. I wish that kid would take a guitar lesson. Swelling, swelling. Aren't you happy, today of all days? Shrinking, shrinking. *Your joy—it shall be unbounded*. Hey, today of all days, can't you be happy? Swelling, swelling.

we? #3

He gets sad when he sees the small room where she slept as a child. The walls are too empty, the windows too large, the floorboards too cold. Alongside those windows, an old-fashioned desk and chest of drawers. Outside those windows, the frigid mountains. At night, the wind delivers a low mournful monologue, squeezing through the spaces around the windows so as to distribute the grief more evenly. Also at night, dead neighbors float up the hill of brambles and hover there, looking in, feasting on the sight of a neighborhood girl all grown up with an East Coast boyfriend now. Lorraine who grew geraniums (everyone's least favorite flower, a stinky flower, Geranium Lorraine they used to call her)—Mr. Mason who made cinnamon doughnuts at Halloween and ceramic eggs at Easter—the Seversons' golden son who was once king of the swim team. Their faces are pale and not unfriendly. But even so. A bit of privacy would be appreciated.

He says, "No offense, but this doesn't seem like the kind of room where a little girl could feel happy or safe." He'd like to do something to it, hang posters of rock bands or Beat poets, replace the white quilt with a tacky flowered comforter, rip CDs and books off tidy shelves until the floor was covered in the crap it ought to be covered in. "Know what I mean?"

She doesn't defend it; it seems silly now to mention all those shameful sentences she wrote in this room, to tell him about the deer and lilac branches and unidentified monsters that sometimes rubbed against the western window, to bring up the night when she stretched the telephone cord and leaned into the northern wall and called someone trembling and trembling spoke to that person until morning.

No, he is not wrong. He's more than right. He's gotten used to her; he knows things about her that she hasn't told him; and this is good. And yet—wasn't it something—to be that lonely—lonely, lonely, as she'll never again be?

we? #4

I'm desperate to know where Bob Dylan is *right now*; maybe he's across the bridge, or across the globe, or maybe he's dying.

Years ago, when we didn't touch each other tenderly except during sex, I sat on the steps while you skateboarded down the sidewalk with a few strangers. It was nighttime. It was springtime. You glided noisily through the darkness. You wore a black sweatshirt with a hood. Your face was a shadow except for your dully gleaming eyes. Because I no longer had your features there before me, I forgot what you looked like. You were slim, strong, impenetrable, incapable of being possessed. I was an explorer, arriving exhilarated at a stone door that wouldn't budge. I tore a silver gum wrapper in half again and again. My heart became a metal bucket, tipping over, saltwater onto sand. Parts of you were lost to me. No matter if I married the person skateboarding darkly through the spring night; he'd never be mine.

Now you lie in a bed, hooked to an IV, your face pale, the room pale. In the aggressive light your face has no shadows. Your bloodshot eyes open and close. I leave for eight minutes and when I return you're almost in tears. You clench my hand in yours, though clench isn't the right word for such frailty. I come close so you can smell me rather than the hospital.

Eventually you joined me on the step. You pinched my shoulder. We didn't yet have methods for expressing the things emerging between us. You shook off your hood and the streetlamp shone orange on you. Though it made me ache, I pulled your hood back up.

I want this to be published so Bob Dylan might read it before he dies. These sentences are the closest I can get to rock 'n roll. How pathetic. This is the closest I can get to a skateboard, a shadowed face. May there be some kind of drums or darkness in the white spaces between the words.

we? #5

Once there was a person whose sadness was so enormous she knew it would kill her if she didn't squeeze it into a cube one centimeter by one centimeter by one centimeter. Diligently, she set about this task. Alone in her room, she grappled with her sadness. It was quite a beast, alternately foggy and slippery; by the time she managed to grip it, her skin was sleek with sweat, soaked with tears. (The sounds coming from her apartment worried the neighbors. *What* was that shy little woman up to?) She twisted her sadness like a dishrag. It strained against her, tugged, pulled. She sat on it to shrink it down the way old-fashioned ladies sat on their snakeskin suitcases.

Then, finally, there it was: a small white cube.

She slipped it into her pocket, went outside, noticed orange lichen growing on tenements, ordered lemonade in a café. The checkered floor nearly blinded her—it looked exactly like joy, and she almost covered her eyes. But instead, she fingered the thing in her pocket. Her eyes became bright prisms; they made her irresistible, and soon she had a friend. One day, passing some kids in the street who had just lost a die down the sewer, she discovered a die in her pocket. "Wow, lady," they said. "Where'dya get a blank one?"

"Gosh," she said, "I really can't remember." And she couldn't.

You know that book where they went all over the world and took pictures of families in front of their homes along with everything they owned? A hut in Kenya, a suburban house in Texas, a Tokyo apartment? I always loved to see the precious and unprecious items, the woven blankets and the TVs, the families standing nervously alongside. Sometimes I look around our home and imagine everything out on the street. But I hope that someday, when they come to take our picture with everything we own, it will just be us, standing before a building, your arm around me, a blank die in my palm.

we? #6

We formulate intricate plans for what to do if we get separated. If you don't make it onto the subway before the doors close, I'll wait in the next station. If you fall in love with someone, I'll poison the tomatoes in her garden. If I fall in love with someone, you'll hammer nails into the wheels of his bicycle. If you leave me, I'll write a book and become famous; when you read it you'll realize I know more about you than you do, and you'll come home. If I leave you, your drawings will garner you a solo show at an important gallery, and I'll become just a person in a damp coat hobbling through rooms full of cruel manifestations of herself, and I'll come home. If I get sad, you'll cover me with leaves until I can't breathe; once I've suffocated sufficiently, you'll unbury me and my infinite grin. If I grow distant, you'll press tacks into the soles of my feet until the color returns to my cheeks. If our baby is born deformed, we'll build a cradle for it out of twigs and moss, like the nests made for infant monsters in medieval times. If you die in a gruesome crunch of metal, I'll locate all your body parts and burn them to ashes; I'll carry you with me in a jam jar that'll always get us held up in customs. If I slice my wrist cutting the potatoes, you'll slice yours cutting the carrots. If I drown in the lake, you'll buy a canoe and paint it white. If I start to see shimmering parakeets when it's just pigeons, you won't give me to the doctors; you'll tell me I'm Duchess and therefore always right. If you lose part of your brain, I'll feed you waffles drowning in syrup, I'll change your diapers, I'll take you to the carnival. If your memory is destroyed, I'll make labels for every single thing in the world. Lamp. Spoon. Hand. Applesauce. Spiderweb. Eyelid. Cup. Tree. You. Me.

the fights

fight #1

A cupcake and a bottle of scotch stood on a subway platform. In the fluorescence, the scotch lacked its rich amber glow. It looked orange and muted, teetering dangerously on the platform's edge. The cupcake pushed the bottle of scotch back to safety, smudging its lavender frosting in the process. To everyone else, the bottle of scotch looked like a drunk young man with bloodshot eyes and a wrinkled shirt; the cupcake looked like a tired young woman with bloodshot eyes and a tense neck. But the bottle of scotch and the cupcake knew they were a bottle of scotch and a cupcake. Embarrassed, the cupcake inched away from the bottle of scotch and stared wistfully at a normal couple. "A cupcake and a bottle of scotch stood on a subway platform. Sounds like the beginning of a bad joke," the cupcake said. "Or a great joke," slurred her companion. "Don't fall, idiot!" the cupcake muttered. "Love me!" the bottle of scotch implored.

A man in a suit and a naked woman stood on a subway platform. In the fluorescence, her limbs looked thick and awkward, but under milder light, she'd be lovely. They embraced. "Goodbye." "Goodbye." "I'll never see you again, will I?" To everyone else, the man in the suit looked like a man in a suit and the naked woman looked like a woman in a dress. But the man in the suit and the naked woman knew he wore a suit while she wore nothing. "Are you cold?" Down the tunnel, the train's howling white eyes.

Long after midnight, I'm awoken by the sound of your shivering body. Yes, it makes an actual sound. I can hear the racket of your bones. Why didn't you get under the covers, idiot? Your body is too drunk to realize how cold it is, so I must realize it for it. Come here, idiot, get in, crawl in, I'll hold you until your blood turns from scotch back into blood, until your bones turn from icicles back into bones.

fight #2

He slams her face into a maple tree until the bark is imprinted in her skin. She becomes a maple tree. He taps her for syrup. She poisons her sap. He falls beside a stream. She becomes the stream. He vomits in the stream. She slaps his face. He feels rejuvenated by the water and goes to punish the tree. She becomes a honeybee and stings him. He yanks her wings off.

She robs a bank and brings the money home. He buys champagne and calls the police. She escapes from prison, finds a glass bottle, and searches for him. He gets a job as a clown. She can't smash him with the bottle while he's surrounded by children. He juggles swords and glares at her. She goes home and crawls into bed.

He sits on her and sings songs with hateful lyrics. She pours boiling water over his sleeping body. He becomes a poisonous teabag in her teacup. She drinks tea and falls into a dead sleep. He drags her to the bathtub and drops the hairdryer in. She gets electrocuted and becomes a ravenous fire. He flees the bathroom. She devours the towels, then pursues him. He becomes a drip on the leaky ceiling. She approaches, radiant flames howling up the walls. He evaporates. She explodes out the front door. He becomes a rainstorm. She races down the block, burning desperately. He mists. She rages through intersections, searching. He drizzles. She sees some litter and, suspecting it's him, burns it. He rains and rains. She realizes the rain is him. He pours down. She leaps up. He smokes and steams. She sputters and gasps.

Two marble statues appear in someone's yard. A man and a woman. They're splendid. A miracle of the Lord. Many poor, sad people come to place marigolds and copper coins at their feet. The marble man and woman gaze at each other with a look that cannot be mistaken. That look—it helps people. Their hearts become strong, and marigolds pile up in the yard.

fight #3

Sometimes a strange man and woman appear in our apartment. They have a terrible marriage. They throw their snakeskin suitcases down in the living room, pop open the brass snaps, and pull out their foolish, expensive clothing. Soon their belongings are strewn over every surface. Clinging to each other, we hide in the corner. Meanwhile, they stride bitterly through the rooms. They fight in the morning and leave for work without apologies, their minds still fizzy with hate. They enjoy hatred, the crazy freedom of it, the delightful abandon, almost like shedding the pull of gravity, taking flight from the stupid safe green earth, no longer handcuffed by the idea of home. They whisper cruel things and leave and return and whisper other, crueler things, their tense jaws no longer serving to muzzle their tongues, words unleashed to punch and pinch. Hate untethers them; they float. They float upward, upward. They cook, but fail to use enough butter. The food turns out dry and unsatisfying. Our plates prefer to jump out of their hands and shatter rather than serve them another meal. Our wineglasses crack rather than enable them to drink. They're forced to buy packaged crackers and cookies; soon there are crumbs everywhere. The desk, the bathtub, the bed— no place is spared the niggling filth of crumbs. They never scrub anything. The counters become sticky with unattended spills, the couch is stained, the coffee table nicked. And still they detest each other. They say, You clean it up. No, you. No, you. No, you. No, you. Even our invincible jade plant withers. Terrified, we curl ourselves into balls and roll ourselves into the closet.

When we reemerge, our plates and wineglasses sit tidily in the cupboard. The jade plant is thriving. The invisible suitcases are gone. The invisible man and woman are gone. We sigh. We go to the bed, where there are no crumbs. For a while, we forget about them. But soon we will begin to prepare ourselves for the next time they come and invade us.

fight #4

Because he sometimes forgets her, she's forced to do certain things, such as pirouette precariously around the apartment. She leaps; she adds flourishes. He keeps reading the newspaper. She abandons her ring on the bureau, but that's not the kind of thing he notices, and, eventually, defeated, she slides it back on. She cooks a five-course dinner that calls for the most expensive spice in the store. This spice is the pollen of a flower, a fact so lovely it makes her whistle the whole way home. She peels each grape with a knife, and by the time the meal is ready her hands are covered with Band-Aids. "Nice," he says afterwards, absentmindedly refolding his napkin, and offers to do the dishes. The next day she carves an ice-sculpture in the kitchen, a life-size likeness of herself. Arriving home after midnight, he does not register the ice girl, except to remark "Gosh, hon, your lips are awfully cold tonight" before heading into the bathroom. The following morning he curses the mysterious puddle in the kitchen that brings him slippingly to the floor. Another morning there's a life-size likeness carved out of chocolate sitting in her chair. Hiding in the closet, she watches him peck the chocolate girl on her sweet melting lips. He says something particularly affectionate as he slides on his sunglasses. Exhausted, she puts away her carving tools. Later, she begs him to accompany her to the park. He comes, irritably. The lake has begun to freeze. Dismayed ducks and indifferent swans drift in the unfrozen areas. She wants him to listen to the sound of the ice broken by the frantic wings of the birds, ice clinking against itself like crystal goblets. A goose, attempting to land with a splash, hits ice instead and slides. He laughs uproariously. "That's not funny!" she says. "It's funny," he counters. "Please," she implores. Then she notices something—the ice has crept all the way to her toes, and below this clear new ice, bright orange leaves are frozen into place.

fight #5

Today Mary looks so cold, so absurdly serene, standing there in the rainy churchyard; finally I approach her. "Hello," I say, "would you like to come inside for tea?" "A nice offer, but wouldn't they miss me?" she says, nodding toward the passersby on the sidewalk. "Oh they won't notice," I lie. "Well," she says hesitantly, "I wouldn't mind tea." Her voice is higher than I'd hoped—I'd been anticipating something deep, rich, chocolaty. With surprising youthfulness, she steps off her pedestal and jumps over the soggy bouquets.

In my kitchen Mary stands awkwardly (and here I'd always assumed she'd make *me* feel awkward). She selects lapsang souchong, the blackest, smokiest tea; I had her pegged as a chamomile girl. Perhaps I've made a mistake. She's not what I expected. "I'm sorry," she murmurs.

With that, my hope returns and I want to tell her everything. "Don't apologize, I'm glad you're here, I have questions for you." She seems relieved; her weird, soft smile reappears. "Mary: do you ever feel like a bar of soap that keeps getting used until it disintegrates into a mushy little bit of nothing?" "Um … no," she says sweetly. "Mary: in springtime I see you when I'm walking home at night. The crabapple trees are puffy pink above you, and behind you the stained glass windows of the rectory shine bright red, and—" "The water's boiling," Mary interrupts. Frustrated, I try again. "Mary: did you see me crying in his arms last Sunday? We were passing by the churchyard, and I was feeling desperate and small and bad and stupid and awkward, and you were standing there so serene, and I—" "Do you have cream?" Mary says. *"Mary: did you see me?"* "I didn't. I'm sorry."

I wish she had a voice like chocolate! But she just drinks tea and cream, happy as a puppy; and when we return to the churchyard, she hurries back to her pedestal, for an angry and mystified crowd is already gathering there, everybody convinced that Mary has failed them.

fight #6

She realizes quite suddenly, many years later, how splendid it was, that day she screamed at him in the street. She sits at an empty, polished table beside a large window in a peaceful neighborhood, drinking water and thinking of it. How swiftly and splendidly the rage had come over her! They'd been walking together; he'd said something; he'd kept walking; she'd stopped; she'd begun to scream. There was a chasm between them, the twelve paces he'd taken without her at his side, and she screamed across it. Her rage was white and clean. It cleared the vision, like an orgasm. She was so correct; every word she screamed was completely correct. She screamed at him in the street, thinking *I am a woman screaming at a man in the street.* Until this very moment, in this quiet room, she's always believed that she was horribly embarrassed by the stares of the passersby. But now it seems obvious that their stares delighted her. She transformed into the uncontrollable woman they assumed she was! He did not love her and never would. She recalls certain things: brown leaves lying on the sidewalk as though they'd been arranged there; an exhausted pink geranium in someone's yard; the windows of the pizzeria; an old woman in a blue coat; a teenage boy with a scared face.

And then, after the outburst?

Well, there's nothing to do but go through with it, stride down the street away from him, shoulders thrown back, your posture absolutely astonishing.

But what about the hours after the encounter, the oncoming night? An unmade bed in a small room, the silence and the gray, a person on the floor, a gulp of leftover peppermint liqueur, the dial tone and the numbers, the black hole of the intestines? It was devastating—sure, devastating, but now it's all so vague. That rage, though!

She sips her water. She strokes the polished table, which gleams in the fading gray light. Oh, she'd do it again! You bet she would. She'd do it again.

fight #7

Something awful has just happened in the kitchen.

If you go in there, you will see that one door in the row of cabinets is open, revealing small bottles of cinnamon, ginger, rosemary, nutmeg, clove, cumin, sage, etc. The refrigerator and the stove are silent. The blender rests dully in its corner. On the countertop, the toaster oven is dark and cold. The gray linoleum of the floor is vaguely sticky underfoot. A jade plant sits on the windowsill. The window is open. Outside, the neighbors' children scream. It is somewhere between dusk and night. Really, it is the time of day when someone ought to turn on a light. The kitchen smells of old dust, spilled orange juice, and the downstairs neighbor's cigarette smoke. It also smells, inexplicably, unpleasantly, of rose perfume. You may wish to hold your breath. In the refrigerator, you will find four eggs in a white bowl. You will find a stick of butter that has not yet thawed, two bags of carrots, half a loaf of brown bread, a nearly empty container of Hershey's chocolate sauce, and three packets of yeast with an expiration date thirteen months ago.

The round table is set for two, with two red placemats, two white bowls, two white plates, two spoons, two forks, two glasses, and two teacups. Also, salt and pepper. One yellow napkin has fallen to the floor. The other yellow napkin lies crumpled on one of the wooden chairs. One glass of water is half full. The other is half empty. The one that is half empty has a chapstick smudge at the top. There is red soup in each bowl. One spoon, unused, has been placed on the plate beneath the soup bowl; the other spoon is up to its neck in uneaten soup. A spinach salad wilts on the table. There is a pot of rice and beans on the stovetop. In the freezer, you will discover outdated peas and a pint of vanilla bean ice cream.

Something awful has just happened here.

fight #8

After several difficult days, they make hot chocolate on the stove, keeping in mind advice once given them by someone: *Use nutmeg, cinnamon, clove, ginger, and cayenne pepper!* Who *was* it? They cannot recall, yet this catalogue of words—rich, mysterious words that they of the microwave dinners scarcely recognize—runs through their minds like a spell. The spices sit on the counter, newly arrived in this bitter little house after a rare expedition to the grocery store. At the store, they were jovial. Lively observations were made about the miraculous ease of obtaining these exotic spices now as opposed to in ancient times. Walking home, they passed trees displaying such weird, brilliant shades of orange that they already felt nostalgic for fall. They heard the weird, mournful call of some migrating bird, but then realized the sound came from a child in a stroller. Suddenly, they became less jovial.

Ok, so. The kitchen. Pan on stovetop. Unsweetened cocoa powder, sugar, five magical ingredients. Pour in water, stir until it becomes a spicy paste. Add milk—yes, whole milk, it has not been easy lately, we need milk that will save us. Heat almost to the boiling point. They feel right then, and righteous, following the unwritten instructions. While the milk is heating, anything's possible. It's possible that this drink will serve as a balm for aching innards. It's possible that someone will turn on the radio and something beautiful will be playing.

But perhaps you, reader, have known all along that this concoction would fail. And indeed: it's bizarrely thick, undrinkably so, in limbo between liquid and solid, powdery lumps of cocoa, cayenne pepper burning the throat, a sickly amount of cinnamon. They attempt to sip a bit, attempt to grin triumphantly at each other. One admits failure with two monosyllabic words; the other quickly agrees, gripping a tense stomach. They have chocolate moustaches and brownish teeth. This does not amuse them. The disappointment is unbearable. They pour it down the sink, but it gets caught in the drain and clings there.

fight #9

I (don't want to think about the morning the wife died from a snake bite, don't want to think about the husband's noisy sadness, don't want to think about the swamps he encountered on his way to hell, don't want to think about the tune he played for the king and queen of hell, don't want to think about the queen turning to the king, don't want to think about the bargain being struck, don't want to think about the wife's imperceptible footsteps as she followed the husband back up through the swamps, don't want to think about the vow he'd made to not look back until, don't want to think about the expectation of joy, don't want to think about the yellow light of the world up ahead, don't want to think about the husband's sudden uncertainty, don't want to think about the vertebrae in his neck enabling him to turn his head, don't want to think about the wife who'd scarcely disrupted the

darkness to begin with now yanked back into darkness)
would prefer to think about an afternoon months beforehand, when they had a little fight in the kitchen;
in their kitchen they had wooden bowls and copper
pots; a jar of honey and a jar of nuts; a basket of plums
and a basket of dried fish; a jug of water and a jug of
wine; a door that opened into the backyard where she
was trying to grow tomatoes, where a gnarled fig tree
stood, where there were honeybees and snakes; what
was the fight about?; if they couldn't even remember
themselves, how can I be expected to know?; but anyway, they had a fight and for some time were irritated;
she stepped outside and he composed a ferocious song;
but then something happened—I'm not sure what—
and they forgot about their fight; someone opened the
door; when I think of them, this is what I think about
rather than thinking about everything else; I think of
a man and a woman in a small house.

fight #10

Once upon a time, a small girl in a dress the color of butter stood on the subway platform. A scowling man pushed her onto the tracks. She hit the third rail. Her dress exploded into flame. Then this small girl found herself beside a lake. There were swans and ducks in the lake, and she began talking to them. The swans made fun of the ducks. The ducks made fun of the swans. They were all having a lovely time. The scowling man appeared from behind a weeping willow and pressed the small girl into the lake until she couldn't breathe. Then this small girl found herself walking down a street lined with old and wonderful trees, and beyond these trees were stately white houses, and in these houses were kind and protective adults whose breath smelled like black pepper and red wine, and these adults held small girls on their laps in the candlelight, and the small girls were entranced by the gleaming satin wallpaper. But this small girl didn't get the chance to enter any of these houses before the scowling man hit her over the head with a croquet mallet.

Then this small girl found herself on the eleventh floor of an abandoned building. All the windows were broken. All the walls had disintegrated. She sat on a dusty oriental rug, and a mirror in a gold frame lay beside her. In that mirror she saw the face of the scowling man. And indeed he was there, standing behind her.

"Hello," she said.

"Darling," the scowling man said, "darling. I am sorry I pushed you off the subway platform. I am sorry I drowned you in the lake. I am sorry I hit you over the head with the croquet mallet. It's just because you never seem one bit frightened—"

"Why don't you shut up," she said, "and let's watch the sunrise?"

Because the abandoned building had no walls, they could see every inch of the rising sun, and they held each other, and were happy.

the failures

failure #1

Before we left for our trip, we neglected to wipe the kitchen counters. Our trip was tiring, and not as much fun as we'd anticipated. When we returned—we gasped—for there—in our kitchen—a mouse carnival was taking place! Our electric mixers made for a wild ride. Our scrub brush wedged against our faucet formed a waterslide. Pearls, once part of our heirloom necklace, served as balls in a lively game. Our cheddar cheese created an edible playground. Some mice had found the scotch and were staggering among the plates. A four-mouse band performed atop the table. They used spoons to keep the beat and mewled cheerfully. It was packed in there. They were all having a great time, wiggling their tails and feasting on the crumbs we'd failed to wipe off the counter. Truth be told, we didn't have it in us to interfere. This was just the kind of party we were always wishing to go to. And now here, in our very own kitchen. . . .

We went to the bedroom . . . and what should

we find there but a nursery, many mother mice nestled among the sheets, each with a bunch of tiny bald sweet things squirming around her. The mother mice smiled—or so it seemed—in the soft yellow light of our bedside lamp. We had to admit, it was a heartwarming scene. Quietly, respectfully, we shut the door behind us.

In the living room, there were no mice. We sat and wondered what to do. And then we noticed that, among our plants on the windowsill, pairs of mice were strolling. They gazed up through the leaves to the enormous moon outside. They nuzzled each other. They sat on the edges of the flowerpots and—perhaps—made plans for the future. It was lovely to behold.

All these mice—the partygoers, the parents, the lovers—they were doing such a better job than we'd ever done. They were succeeding where we'd failed again and again . . . we gathered up our luggage, headed toward the door, and went away forever.

failure #2

A girl living in the modern world decides she would like to go dancing. She pictures herself in an enormous room with black-and-white checkered floors and crystal chandeliers—wearing high heels that make her legs look ten feet long—a crimson dress that twirls up to reveal her underwear—she dances with everyone and everyone dances with her—everyone smiles at her, and everyone winks—they stand back to watch her spin—these people are all so delightful that even when they leave the dance floor to go to the bathroom they keep the beat in their fingers and toes—their joy is unbounded.

This girl begins to dress herself. Her practical modern shoes and skirt are not the joyous garments she envisioned, but. Leaving the concrete room where she lives, she pinches her cheeks to give them the flushed color of a dancing girl's. Out in the streets of the city, she searches for a place where she can go dancing. She asks a woman in a tracksuit; the woman turns away as though she's been addressed by a crazy person. She asks a man with two briefcases; he smiles sadly and grips more tightly the handles of his briefcases. The streets are gray and quiet, the bars subdued. She asks a lady pushing a baby carriage; this lady laughs unkindly before turning her attention back to the infant. She asks a skeletal policeman, who, with great confidence, gives her directions to a nearby address.

Grateful, tempted to kiss his hand, the girl follows the policeman's instructions, only to find herself in front of a Chinese takeout restaurant. She leans her face against the corner of the brick building. *If only I could trade places with my great-great-grandmother, who surely must have danced in a crimson dress beneath crystal chandeliers on black-and-white—* After a long while, she moves away from the brick building. Unbeknownst to her, the bricks and mortar have left a dramatic and disturbing imprint in her cheek; all the way home, she looks as though something terrible has just happened to her.

failure #3

We harbor certain titillating feelings toward the blind woman in the neighborhood. Overtaking her on the sidewalk, we become aware of the length and shapeliness of our legs, and the ease with which we move. The blind woman inches along, relying on her pole, like some weird cautious creature on the ocean floor. We notice things about her, such as the fact that she always wears khaki trousers with a brightly colored shirt. We agree that khaki matches everything, and that it is wise, if you are blind, to wear only khaki trousers. She has one pair of shoes; these shoes have thick black soles, and are the same kind our mothers used to force us to buy. Another fact about the blind woman, which sounds like it comes from a heartwarming movie: she always has this little smile on her face.

Eventually, you lose interest in the blind woman. She becomes just another odd fixture of the neighborhood, like the telephone booth covered in graffiti that says *You love me You love me* and the statue on the church's lawn in which Mary has the body of a hot teenage girl.

Whenever I overtake the blind woman, I wonder if she can smell me. If so, what do I smell like? Like the cocoa butter cream I put on this morning, or like the sex we had yesterday? Are her nostrils offended by the onions I ate at lunchtime? I wonder if she can hear me, if she recognizes the sound of my gait, if my heavy breathing deceives her into believing I'm a man. I wonder if she thinks of me as a familiar and comforting presence.

Once, I spotted dog shit on the pavement in front of her.

"Look out!" I said.

But she didn't know I was talking to her, and she stepped gracefully over it, smiling, and I wondered if it was her sense of smell that did the trick, and I wondered what kind of bitch would say "Look out" to a blind woman.

failure #4

We count nine oranges on the highway below us. How bright they look in our gray city. Standing on the overpass, we cling to the fence. We peer through. How radiant those oranges are, flickering among the fast cars. We have not seen oranges in many months. In fact, it is rather amazing that we recognize them at all, considering how unsophisticated we are. We tell ourselves we must be geniuses. Who spilled them, we wonder. Was it an accident? Did they fall from an enormous truck driven all night from nice green swampy Florida? Or did some carload of rich people get bored with their oranges and throw them out the window? What asshole could get bored of oranges? We dare one another to go down there and—

Just then, a charter bus pounds over the fifth orange. It is flattened, surrounded by a wet smear of orange juice, which we glimpse whenever there's a gap between cars. Then the second orange meets with the same fate, and the eighth orange too. We think to ourselves how similar blood and orange juice are, in this context. Our teachers have criticized us for this. They have informed us that we suffer from the pathetic fallacy. Wow, we say. That is so mean. How can you say that to us? No, the teachers reply. It's not as bad as it sounds. It just means—it just means that you tend to attribute human emotions to inanimate objects.

Well, anyway, the oranges are bleeding on the highway.

We long for oranges. We start to believe that if we'd gotten them, if those oranges on the highway had made their way into our mouths, we would have been better than we are. The scabs on our mosquito bites would have vanished; our sneakers would be clean again; we'd feel less tired and less hot. We'd be smarter, kinder, stronger, more admirable. We'd no longer be filled with this unbearable sadness at the sight of things such as nine oranges smashed on the highway.

failure #5

Our bodies have no memory of the seasons. If they did, we'd never stay in the same place; if the cruelty of February and the cruelty of August could play simultaneously over our skin, we'd go mad. We'd leave our homes, board southbound buses, wouldn't stop till we reached eternal primavera. Thankfully, our bodies are forgetful. They enjoy the strange shocking brightness of spring and fall, then talk themselves into staying for another season.

We go to the primeval park where our prehistoric ancestors can be seen. The path leads down into a canyon. The blackberries are so big they make us laugh. Also we're laughing because we're frightened, and nervous. What will they be like, these ancestors of ours? Won't they wish to attack, and won't they win? Reeds thick as thumbs grow everywhere. Then we spot one, squatting beside a shallow stream, its hand— yes, opposable thumbs!—outstretched to grab a frog. Its limbs are thicker and shorter than ours. It has a hump on its back. Its hair is stringy. We feel little affiliation with it. Only as much as might be felt with a cow. Its face is more like the face of a beast than like one of our faces. Suddenly, it becomes aware of us. Or perhaps, like any non-human creature, it has been aware of us all along, our expensive hiking boots grinding deafeningly into the reeds, and has just now chosen to acknowledge us. We can tell, when it looks at us, that the latter is true. It looks at us with such compassion! We become shy, and retreat.

One thing we cannot forget, even years later, is the skin of that creature. It was a warm dark golden color, thick and smooth, durable as plastic—skin capable of remembering the seasons, skin that could bear February and August simultaneously. That body was not forgetful. Those eyes absorbed in minute detail each of our scared, amazed faces. Guiltily, we wonder why we won, and why we have covered the entire globe with our discontent.

failure #6

Once upon a time, there was a can of cheap beer on a small round plastic table on a porch by a lake in Maine. (Mosquitoes swarmed in the orange beam cast by the single porch light on the red and gold can of beer. It was a hot moonless night in August. Someone was saying something, an old man educating a boy or an old woman chiding an old man. There were no banjos. They had all gone home, and the harmonicas too. It was just the can of cheap beer in the orange mosquito light on the table on the porch in the summer in Maine. One half of the can was illuminated. The other half was shadowed. The label was gold and ornate with red cursive lettering. The can itself was red. Seven mosquito bites swelled on an arm. The lake made dark sounds. Later, the beer can was tossed down a dark stairway into a basement bin; it hovered briefly, gleaming in a slim slab of orange light from the light bulb on the porch, before dropping and hitting many other cans.)

Decades later, whenever he hears the word "nostalgia," this is what he sees: a can of cheap beer in orange light. Was it one night, or many that blur into one?

In the new millennium, they add a wing to the museum: The Hall of Nostalgia. This exhibition is immediately popular. There are life-size dioramas of beautiful farm-girls milking cows—press a button to hear the sound of fresh milk hitting a tin pail—and young men on ladders in an orchard, throwing fruit down into baskets, one gleaming apple suspended permanently in midair. Every corner he turns he half-expects to see a small, dark diorama: a single orange light bulb, a plastic table, a can of beer.

On an afternoon in August in a bed in a city, an inconsolable woman cries quietly. He tells her the most comforting story in the world: Once upon a time, there was a can of cheap beer.

failure #7

In the American Museum of Natural History, in the year 20—, we come upon the Hall of the North American Environment, but between ourselves we call it the Hall of Nostalgia for Things We Have Never Seen. There are, for instance, dioramas the size of shoeboxes; each portrays one of the four seasons, but none of these scenes is familiar. When was autumn a mule pulling a cart through orange leaves down a dirt road alongside a stone wall past fields yellow with wheat under branches dragged downward by apples beneath a pure blue sky, the cart itself loaded with wicker baskets of apples? Oh darling diorama-maker. Don't you know we've never tasted freshly picked apples? When was winter a frozen lake, a group of children with ice skates, a farmhouse releasing smoke into a white sky, heaps of snow tenderly covering the barn and the hills? Was spring ever really this green, I ask you, you diorama-maker, you who painted this optimistic lavender sky, you who conceive of slender white birches, you who still believe in daffodils and in the grass? And wouldn't everyone have died of joy at the height of this summer you've brought us? Oh yes we can hear the crickets, my dear diorama-making friend, we can smell the hot smell of skin warmed by the sun, we can smell the dark smell of algae in a pond encrusted with lily pads, we can, we can, we can feel the long marks left by the extravagant grass on our bare legs. Radiant dragonflies, mating, skim the dark water. Raspberries on the bush ripen before our eyes. Oh oh.

You should not have brought all this to mind.

Because now, you see, aching, we leave the Hall of the North American Environment. We become aware, once again, of the air-conditioning chilling our blood. Unlike the good farmer and the good farmer's wife, we do not stay near each other for warmth. No; we pass through the great synthetic doors and into the searing steel city without touching.

the far-flung families

far-flung family #1

Long ago, my father built a covered wagon. He filled it with practical things, such as guns and ammunition and a bellows, and with less practical things, such as rose-seeds and a rocking chair. My mother climbed into this wagon beside him. They headed due west.

At night, they dreamed of New England, of green fields and huge trees and stone walls and white houses with black shutters and the rum cake made by my mother's mother and that hot heavy green smell the air takes on in summertime. During the day, they passed brown expanses of land, snarls of barbed wire, and, occasionally, a mud house. They ate snakes. Their noses ran with dust and blood. My mother became pregnant and began to ache.

After several hundred years, my parents arrived at the Rocky Mountains. My father built a house. My mother planted rose-seeds. Their parents started to seem unreal to them, the disembodied recipients and senders of infrequent letters. The dry noise of aspen leaves was the first sound I ever heard. My sisters and I grew up without shoes, hardening our dusty feet, always somewhat thirsty. So effortless was our happiness that it was years before we understood the difference between happiness and sadness.

As teenagers, we began to wonder about New England. Our parents had told us tales of pure white houses on lawns so green our imaginations couldn't imagine them. Eventually, a train ticket was bought. On the train, I dreamed of the Rocky Mountains, of aspen leaves and shallow streams containing flecks of fool's gold and sunsets that made your eyes throb. Upon my arrival, I noticed a hot heavy smell, a green smell, and my face felt moister than ever before. I was taken out to tea, and given a cucumber sandwich, and a tiny rum cake, and I drank from a china cup painted with roses. I sipped tea from a distant continent; and suddenly my parents started to seem unreal to me, the disembodied recipients and senders of infrequent emails.

far-flung family #2

The king's daughter goes to live in a faraway city with the clever yet dirty craftsman who (unbelievably!) completed the challenges necessary to win her hand. There, she learns coarse language and forgets how to write perfect script. Her letters are messy and joyful. She wants her father to visit. He's a wonderful king. He used to yank trees out of the ground and lay them on their sides, exposing a hundred years' worth of roots, in order to teach her important botanical facts. She already knows what they will do when he comes. . . .

She leads the king over the huge bridge with the double archways. The city glows strangely. They go deep into Chinatown and eat unrecognizable foods. They wander up avenues. The king sees many people. The air smells of exhaustion, car exhaust, women's perfumes, roasting nuts, warm sewers. She's ashamed that it doesn't smell clean here. She buys him hot cashews. She buys him water. She gives money to any street performer—a violinist, a tangoing couple, a blue clown—that causes any reaction in his face. She wishes to guard him from hunger, thirst, danger, discomfort, boredom, dog shit, to direct his gaze always and only toward beautiful things. They go to the library where the ceiling is painted to resemble blue skies and to the train station where the ceiling is painted to resemble night skies. The whole day they crane their necks upward. This is no forest stroll, eyes cast downward to spot caterpillars and poison ivy and intricate root systems. She worries about him, checks his eyebrows for signs of dismay, holds his arm. When evening comes, she takes him back to her small home in a taxicab. She makes stew. She makes herbal tea. She arranges a bed for him on the floor, piling on too many blankets. She speaks in a tranquil voice to mitigate the sound of sirens.

But the king never comes. He stalks through his forest, ripping trees out of the ground, crushing columbines, scaring magpies and scaring deer.

far-flung family #3

A very famous man is being paid a large sum of money to make a speech to an enormous crowd. Already they are clapping for him. It is almost time for him to stride out onto the stage, and adjust the microphone, and talk, and gesture toward a screen where important messages will be projected.

Yet this man, standing behind the curtain, suddenly wants nothing more than to be in a small bathroom. The image of this bathroom floods his mind. It is not a bathroom he has ever seen before. It is quite small, only a narrow sink beside a toilet and a single window, no bathtub or shower. It is infused with clean blue light. The floor is tiled black and white. The walls are white. The toilet is white. The lid of the toilet is down. The sink has two knobs, H and C.

He does not need to urinate or defecate, nor does he feel the urge to vomit. The desire for the bathroom is not a practical one. It is just that he wants to be there, in that quiet clean blue light, near to the white walls, the white toilet, the white sink. He adds flourishes: a round bar of almond soap, a rack containing one thin white towel, the greenery of a lilac bush on the other side of the window.

Still they are clapping for him. The time has come for him to stride out onto the stage; the time has come, and it has passed, and he has not stridden out onto the stage. The people backstage are getting worried; because he is so famous, they keep their voices calm; they ask him if he wouldn't mind please going out now, because it is time.

In the small bathroom you cannot hear anything except the occasional dripping of the faucet. If you examine the sink, you will find a green streak beneath the H knob, which is the knob that drips. This green streak is a mysterious color; an indescribable smear.

far-flung family #4

Some stupid drunk girls get kicked out of a nightclub. They wobble down the alleyway beside the black and filthy canal. One of the girls, upon seeing the black water, suddenly starts feeling a feeling she doesn't know the word for (nostalgia). Hey, she says, when I was like a little girl I like thought I was a mermaid. Two girls begin vomiting behind a dumpster. Can you like even believe that? she says. The golden charm bracelet of the nearest vomiting girl falls off her wrist and into her vomit and she starts crying. I like totally believed my real parents were a mermaid and like a merman, and someday they'd come and like take me away, she says. The other girls vomit or try to find their cell phones or wonder stupidly where they can hail a cab. I thought my mermaid parents would like get into the house through the bathtub drain so I would like sit on the edge of the bathtub and wait for them. She hoists herself dangerously onto the concrete embankment of the canal. Just like this, she says, I'd like sit on the bathtub just like this. I was like positive they'd come and give me back my mermaid tail and finally I could go and live in the ocean and be like happy. The girls are done vomiting and the one girl has forgotten about her golden charm bracelet and another girl has found her cell phone and a girl who is slightly less drunk than the others says they can't hail a cab here since it's like an alleyway so the stupid drunk girls start wobbling toward an actual street, but they are too drunk to remember that girl who like thinks she's a mermaid. She's left there, on the concrete embankment beside the canal, and she starts getting happy, thinking of how cool and beautiful the ocean will feel; eagerly she awaits the single strong blue arm that will rise up out of the black canal just before dawn.

far-flung family #5

Picturing dirty canals and infinite traffic jams and boulevards blowing with garbage and dangerous curses spray-painted on inaccessible walls, my parents still refuse to visit New York City, so I am forced to lie. Painstakingly, I write my childhood address on an envelope, attempting to imitate the babyish bubbliness that once characterized my handwriting, hiding all traces of the strong, dark, harsh script I've developed since I left.

My dears: I assure you you've got it all wrong. In the harbor near Wall Street (where the water is *not* covered with oily rainbows), there are many pretty little houses on stilts. Yes, sweet little houses painted turquoise, red, canary yellow. Perhaps you've never heard of them? Well, it's a recent phenomenon, and maybe such news doesn't travel 1,800 miles, but I swear they exist! Darling families live in these stilt-houses. They hang ferns and violets from the porches, and call out merrily to the people on shore. Their children dream of crawling through the arteries of whales as through playground tunnels. When you come, we'll go and wave at them. The sun will glimmer across the greenish water. We'll be happy. We'll walk up Manhattan, which *isn't* entirely paved over. Roundabout Chelsea, the streets give way to dirt roads. It's positively wild there! Vines and magnolias arch overhead, sieving the orange sunlight. There are yellow frogs and red turtles. Noisy creeks run beneath wooden bridges. Artists live hidden among the blackberry bushes in wooden shacks with geraniums planted in the kitchen floor and hand-sewn quilts for doors. We'll stroll along, laughing and joking. If you slip off a footbridge, I'll pull you up out of the dark rich muck and the poison ivy. It'll be so fun. We'll sit on a log, examining toadstools. Please visit. I'll make it pleasant for you. I swear I'll take you to nice places. Still Yours—Helen.

I have one stamp. Appropriately, it depicts an orchid. I take the letter down the block (through blowing garbage, past resplendent graffiti, beneath oily fumes) to the mailbox.

far-flung family #6

Yet again I find myself obliged to defend myself. I didn't realize what would happen! I swear that when I put my old clothes out on the sidewalk it was a soft, sweet morning. I was desperate to have them claimed by strangers and enter other homes where they could become more fully themselves.

When the wind rose I was on the telephone, telling him things such as "Sometimes I'm like a screaming woman in a locked room" and "Sometimes I'm like a woman wearing a muzzle." Hanging up, I observed huge trees swaying as though they were saplings. It was then that I remembered my clothes. Rushing outside into swirling yellow pollen, I sneezed nine times and my eyes took on a yellow hue. I saw what I'd feared: twisted, floppy, yellow with pollen, my clothes lay in the street, shipwrecked sailors clinging to an inhospitable shore. They looked familiar, of course, but also strange, like an ex you haven't seen in half a decade. Perhaps that's why I left them—yes, I'll admit it,

I left them strewn there in the street. Who knew what would become of them? Nobody would want them now, that was certain; yet I did not reclaim them.

Forgive me.

My mother, stricken suddenly with the urge to contact each of her children, called from across the continent. A knot in her stomach, she claimed, convinced her that something awful had happened. This, from the woman who taught me to say things such as "Sometimes I'm like a screaming woman." I assured her that nothing awful had happened. Hanging up, I was filled with regret; I should have told her the truth. But the truth comes in several forms, and none seems quite appropriate: (a) "This morning I thought my arm was stretched across his body, but in fact it was lying numbly asleep upon my own torso," (b) "It's tremendously windy here; the treetops soon may fall," (c) "All my old clothes are sprawled out there in the middle of the street."

far-flung family #7

Thank God we're going digital, because the thought of all the printed photographs in the world lying in albums and piled in drawers is quite vexing to me! How many thousands of photographs of the Eiffel Tower, the Pyramids, the Grand Canyon, the Great Wall, the Taj Mahal, does this world need? I drown in the knowledge of so many photographs being taken every day. I envision them in albums that will be looked at a handful of times until the end of time. Meanwhile, the world gets heavier and heavier with the weight of redundant photographs. But it's not tourist sights alone. Photographs of mother and child just after birth, baby's first steps, first day of school, birthdays, graduations; billions of brides and grooms with strained grins.

Dear humankind, why do you need to capture it all from every angle? It's always the same, always! The mother's tired smile, the graduate's hopeful face, etc. You'd save yourself so much trouble by acknowledging that what happens to you happens to everyone; for any event you wish to commemorate there are already *too many photographs.*

"Stop, Paul! Please stop!" my mother said as each family trip wore on and my father kept taking photographs. A photograph of me in the hotel room, my face puffy and stupid with sleep. A photograph of stray dogs down an alleyway. A photograph of my mother saying "Stop, Paul! Please STOP! When will we ever look at these."

Once I discovered a box of photographs on a shelf in my parents' closet. Why hadn't these made it into the albums through which I occasionally glanced? Then I saw that in each of the photographs, my older sister looked normal. She looked like a normal, normal baby! Her eyes focused on the lens. She wasn't wringing her hands. Her chin wasn't shiny with saliva. Her spine didn't yet curve and cramp her. She wore smocked dresses, hand-wash only. She beamed in my mother's lap, clung to my father's chest. The camera— the precious, deceitful camera—had witnessed it.

far-flung family #8

A horrible mistake has been made. Each year, I see my parents for a few summer days, a few winter days. Aside from that we're connected by tenuous things—telephones that flicker in and out of service, poorly punctuated emails. My parents sit on a deck in the faraway mountains. They sip coffee while above them swallows dip and whir. It used to be that on such mornings their offspring would eventually awake, come out onto the deck, see the swallows.

Sometimes it simultaneously rains, snows, sleets, and drizzles in this city. We imagine apocalypse. Sidewalks flooding, subways stalled. In the churchyard, the plastic angel malfunctions. Her electrical wings make mournful, mechanical sounds. People stand in long, meaningless lines. Someone growls, and everyone wonders, *Who's growling?*

It won't be easy to get to the mountains when apocalypse comes. We'll go on foot, walking west along empty highways until our first pair of shoes wears out, our second, our third. We'll get skinny and start to resemble animals. Language will elude us. Nothing could have prepared us for this. My parents tried to prepare me, difficult hungry childhood camping trips, blisters and insects. I'll have to thank them. Will they be on the deck when we arrive? Will they have coffee to spare, and unpolluted swallows? Will my child be born in my childhood home? Will we build a family settlement with outbuildings and a protective log wall? Will we coax apple trees and wheat out of the hillside? Will my brother arrive from the North with a stolen cow? Will my sister arrive from the South with a loom? Will my parents grow old and happy, grateful for the apocalypse?

In another version of this story, we die on the road, murdered for our shoes, or simply sinking from dehydration into oblivion, or killed by sadness at the sight of a dead child. In yet another version, my parents are not alive when we arrive. They are corpses, embracing in their big old bed. My brother never arrives, nor my sister.

far-flung family #9

Once, long ago, there were many things that brought comfort in the morning: A heavy rain falling. A large tree swaying. A small wooden bed. The distant sound of a man's voice and a woman's voice, exchanging occasional words. The smell of someone cooking breakfast elsewhere. Gray light at the window. The green weight of summertime. Clover growing between gravestones encrusted with orange lichen. An old wedding dress hanging in a closet. The closet door ajar. A metal fan whirring. Four raccoons walking along the telephone wire. Paper dolls preserved behind picture frames. A wooden jewelry box painted red, a strand of yellow beads, and a rusty broach.

Now, there are many things that bring uneasiness in the morning: A heavy rain falling. A large tree swaying. A small wooden bed. The distant sound of a man's voice and a woman's voice, exchanging occasional words. The smell of someone cooking breakfast elsewhere. Gray light at the window. The green weight of summertime. Clover growing between gravestones encrusted with orange lichen. An old wedding dress hanging in a closet. The closet door ajar. A metal fan whirring. Four raccoons walking along the telephone wire. Paper dolls preserved behind picture frames. A wooden jewelry box painted red, a strand of yellow beads, and a rusty broach.

Who said 'Nature reflects the colors of the soul'? I should like to live alongside a pond with whoever said that. Sometimes the mosquitoes would annoy us, and sometimes they wouldn't. His soul would feel dirty and clean and dirty and clean again, and my soul would too.

Someone says: 'You should not be so melancholy.' Someone replies: 'It's true. I should not be so melancholy.' Someone says: 'You are not easy.' Someone replies: 'It is frightening to be a wife.' Someone says: 'For crying out loud.' Someone replies: 'I'd rather not go to bed sad, if you don't mind.' Someone says: 'I don't mind.' Someone replies: 'I'd rather not wake up uneasy.' Someone says: 'For crying out loud. Look out at that beautifully falling rain!'

the envies

envy #1

My sister and I are jealous of the girls in Maxfield Parrish paintings. We, too, want to stroll down marble staircases, a cliff on one side and a palace on the other. We want to live among roses of indescribable shades and fountains running with snowmelt water in light that's always like daybreak or sundown. We want to wear white fabrics that cling longingly to our hips. How unencumbered one's body must feel in that cool golden air! We wish to sleep outside, and be woken by naked androgynous children.

There have been brief moments—once, at dusk, coming upon a faux Greek colonnade in a city park, we managed to disregard the graffiti, and sat there, and were happy. Another time, in another city park, there was a waterfall, the black stillness of the pond disrupted by the extravagance of white bubbles. But then the breeze blew, bearing the smell of chlorine rather than the cardamom fragrance of Arcadia, and we were disappointed.

Also there was a time years ago, when we were children and our parents took us to see the strange red cliffs of Utah. My sister sat dangerously at the edge of a cliff and I stood behind. I still had thick hair then; the wind pushed it and the sun transformed it to copper. Our limbs were lithe, our skin golden.

This happened long before we'd ever heard of Maxfield Parrish. Imagine our surprise when, as teenagers, we discovered a painting of two golden-skinned girls on a red cliff, their copper hair twisted by the wind, one girl sitting, the other standing behind!

Now my sister and I live in large frightening cities on opposite coasts, and we have learned that Maxfield Parrish paintings are not to be taken seriously.

We are so jealous of the girls in Maxfield Parrish paintings! We're desperate to live on a cliff together. We want to have honeycrisp apples and cream for breakfast, and walk among gardenias and waterfalls, and let the sun warm the lonesomeness out of our veins.

envy #2

The colonists on the ship that brought the first honey-bees to the New World suffered a worse passage than all other colonists. In addition to everything—stenches, storms, sunburns, hunger, thirst, constipation, nostalgia, insomnia, uncertainty, cold moons on black waters, the desperate yearning for sugar, the infuriating weight of one's body, its tyrannical needs, how heavily it moors one to the stinking wooden boards, preventing one from experiencing other, more abstract desires—they're subjected to bee-stings, most earthbound and gardenbound of sufferings, a pain historically mitigated by the aroma of peaches, grass, dirt, roses, usually forgotten by the time the sunbeams turn to honey, warmly recalled as the worst mishap of a perfect day (and anyhow aren't honeybees responsible for peaches, roses, the metaphor of honey?), but there's nothing in this waterbound world to mitigate the pain, and so they howl, howl until gender and age vanish and each becomes just a creature, howling. Meanwhile, a tiny golden carcass falls to the salty boards.

The colonists get stupid, their minds drifting in dumb directions due to the lack of sugar in their diets. They wonder how the bees manage to stay on board if they're always flying. Why doesn't the ship just sail out from under them? And what's this peculiar continent ahead where, supposedly, there are no honeybees? It doesn't sound like a place hospitable to stone houses with rose trellises . . . nostalgia returns, and uncertainty, before giving way to hunger, constipation.

How does the beekeeper keep his shirt so white? *Why* doesn't he develop sunburns? He picks the bee up, places it in his palm, flicks it into the ocean. The golden carcass glimmers midair. The night the sugar-starved colonists try to break into the hive to get at the honey, he exhibits superhuman strength. Furiously, they wonder: *Why don't the bees sting him?*

In fact, they do sting him, but he doesn't mind. The bees build an orchard in his brain. He dwells there. He envisions the continent ahead, covered with orchards, shimmering with bees.

envy #3

Once upon a time, a person walked through an orchard on a hill. It seemed to this person that the air smelled of cinnamon, though upon further reflection the illusion of cinnamon could be accounted for by the fact that apples are so often served with cinnamon. And indeed there were apples of all kinds—Macoun, Honeycrisp, Braeburn, Baldwin, Jonagold—rotting very sweetly in the grass. From the top of the hill, one could see many other hills, which resembled medieval tapestries woven of maroon and umber thread. Also at the top: Dirt wagon tracks. A yellow farmhouse. A vegetable garden. For the first time ever, this person was not envious of all the other, happier people who were surely enjoying themselves in other, more beautiful places. Yes, this person knew there was no one of whom to be jealous for these few minutes!

This person strolled toward an exceedingly fruitful tree. In fact, its overloaded upper branches had begun to rip its trunk apart with their weight. This person stared at it, trying to decide if it was a symbol of lushness or of death. This person ducked under the branches of the tree. There, one could see only four colors: blue sky, green leaves, gray bark, red apples. It may sound like an oversimplification, but the world *is* simple beneath an apple tree.

This person noticed one apple in particular, and recalled a fact: infants are attracted to faces that are perfectly symmetrical. This person stretched up to pick the symmetrical apple. It became impossible not to think of Eve. It seemed possible that, upon twisting the apple off the branch, upon tearing into it with one's teeth, thunder would shake the orchard and an angry grandfather would awaken. But. Of course. Nothing happened. Just: a sudden swift return to the conviction that other, happier people were right now enjoying other, more beautiful places. And also: a sudden swarm of gnats, rising from nowhere, swirling around the mouth that bit the apple, attempting to enter the nostrils and the eyes.

envy #4

I am jealous of them.

They are sitting there together on the rain-darkened dock in the honeyed sunlight of an October afternoon. Sixteen leaves in different shades of orange have fallen onto the dock. Her hair is just the right color, halfway between brown and blonde. He will age well. They have two mugs and two cups. One thermos and one basket. Thirty-three grapes, one loaf of bread, one plaid blanket. They wear four leather shoes, two pairs of jeans, two tan overcoats. Beyond them, the lake reflects the forest—smears of red, yellow, dark green in the green water. They are sensible people, and say sensible things to each other. They make astute, amusing observations about the world. Love comes easily to them. They do not falter; they do not have doubts. They invest in the stock market, do important work during the weeks, and relax on the weekends. He adores her. She feels adored; in response, she becomes the loveliest woman ever. She laughs at something he says. She sips something from her mug.

Though this is just the photograph on the cover of the L.L. Bean catalogue, still I can smell the damp blackberry bushes alongside the lake. I know every inch of the scene is manicured, from the flawless grapes to the friendly bend in his knee, from the sixteen fallen leaves to the chemistry between them; but still I am jealous. For however long the photo shoot lasted, that man and that woman sat together on a rain-darkened dock with trees turning red and yellow all around them. For a brief time, it might as well have been true: the tranquility of the lake, the comfort of a mug held between two hands, the tenderness with which he gazed at her, the peace in her eyes.

Those who achieve even five minutes of such perfection—mediated or no—deserve our envy. The world is a humid and difficult place, and we are so often exhausted, and love is strange, and arrives in stops and starts.

the mistakes

mistake #1

A man comes into a party. A woman at the party once knew him and he once knew her. Initially they don't recognize each other. There are many people. It is too hot. The white wine in the fridge has somehow gotten warm. He holds a plastic cup in his large hand. She leans against the mantelpiece but her elbow slips. She stands with her hands clasped in front of her. It was a long time ago. It was only one night. She was wearing a long blonde wig. She'd been in a play about a mermaid. Neither of them had cared either way.

She says: "I sometimes think of you because I've recently met someone who reminds me of you." For the first time since his arrival the man does not look bored. He says: "Oh? Who?"

Then the thing that's been happening to the woman lately happens again. Parts of her mind are suddenly lost to her. She leans against the mantelpiece again and her elbow slips again. She tries to recall their conversation. She said 'I sometimes think of you because

I've recently met someone who reminds me of you' and he said 'Oh? Who?' But now she wonders: Who indeed? She cannot think of anyone who reminds her at all of this man. She cannot think of anyone she has met recently. She never meets anyone. To whom, then, had she been referring?

The woman grinds her faux pearls together in her palm. The man twists his thick neck around. Someone ought to buy an air-conditioner. He has recently become a lawyer. The woman realizes that she definitely does not sometimes think of him. She hasn't ever thought about him. She does not know anyone who reminds her of him.

She says: "Actually, the person I was thinking of is you. I just ran into you at this party, and seeing you reminded me of you."

Then she dumps her wine on his foot to distract him from how odd she is but he's already left.

mistake #2

At times, we wake hopeful, sensitive to good omens, such as the cotton-candy seller who sits down beside us on the subway, puffs of cotton-candy guarding our heads like an umbrella; such as the inexplicable fireworks glimpsed over faraway skyscrapers on a boring night in June.

Like tribal peoples, we obey the imperative of these omens. We dress ourselves in brightly colored garments. We load blankets and games, water and food, into a wheelbarrow. We go to the city park, we spread blankets, we shuffle a deck of cards, we wait for our friends to arrive. We put our trust in the city lake, which reflects a half-blue sky; we put our trust in the grass. We become convinced that we will be able to create the impression of Arcadia, of nymphs and gods lounging in some clean and wild place, how pastoral it will all be, how softly the weeping willow dips seven fingers into the lake, you may think those are scraps of litter but in fact they are clusters of small white flowers.

We sit there on our blanket, awaiting joy.

Our friends appear, smoking cigarettes and worrying about the weather. With yellowed fingers, they point out the black cloud we've neglected to notice. Unlike them, we are brave. We are not afraid of lightning, nor thunder. In fact, we rather enjoy such things. We swear to—

But at the first drops of rain, we grab the blankets and the games; we push the wheelbarrow through the downpour; our friends follow behind in a long lackadaisical line. We try to think of our life as a moveable feast. We try to yelp with the thrill of the rain. Our kitchen fills with damp cigarette smoke. Wet heels grind crumbs into our carpet; someone writes something in pen on the fabric of our couch.

Hours later, cleaning up, throwing plastic cups away, we become furious with ourselves for misinterpreting the signs. We should have kept the blankets safely in the linen closet. We should have built an ark.

mistake #3

It was a dark and dangerous time. Failures of both large and small magnitude took place regularly. Still, someone—charmed by our youth if not our cleanliness—gave us a hundred-dollar gift certificate to a fine restaurant. Trying to disregard the alarming rumors we'd been hearing—my cousin's husband had taken to shitting in the bathtub, your aunt had taken to threatening her dog with a medieval dagger—we wiped the grime off our faces. We adorned my head with stolen flowers and found a necktie in a dumpster. But youth is beautiful, and they led us graciously into the restaurant. Perhaps they assumed we'd paid a lot for our ragged clothing. Ashamed of the flowers wilting behind my ear, I went to the ladies' lounge. The toilets were golden. Beside the sink lay linen cloths finer than anything we owned. Back at the draped table, I sat up and tried not to feel humble, but looking at you—your bloodshot eyes, your poorly shaven chin—made me feel humble all over again. Knowing nothing, we said yes to everything the waiter offered.

Once the wine arrived in its bucket of ice, things improved. We began to feel not only comfortable with this kind of luxury, but even deserving of it. The courses came one by one, combinations we scarcely understood—grapefruit with *licorice*? yam with *lemongrass*? *raspberry chamomile* duck? We couldn't keep them straight while we ate, couldn't recall them once we'd finished. But the food didn't matter, we assured ourselves. It was everything else that mattered, the waiter's patient smile, the second bottle of wine being uncorked, the way we looked rich in the candlelight. Yes, we could get used to this. We forgot about our small bed, our clunking refrigerator.

When the check arrived on its golden clipboard, it said: $1114. We laughed at the decimal point error. The dear waiter returned. We pointed out the mistake. He regarded us mournfully. Our blood turned black and cold, rushing around our brains and stomachs; we left that place with nothing to call our own.

mistake #4

We're not the kind of people who take taxicabs. Instead, we march down midnight streets damp and shiny with gasoline, over canals releasing black fog, past the lot where taxicab drivers doze. How yellow and faithful the taxicabs look! The whole world drips with rain and anxiety, but the taxicabs are safe.

A bleak block beyond, we come upon it, there beside the superhighway. Long ago, it would have been one of many mansions lining a boulevard. Now it looms here alone, blackened with car exhaust, no buffering gateway between the sidewalk and its front steps.

We'd scrub the outside until the original color was revealed. We'd repair the leaks. We'd pull down the stained wallpaper. We'd bring in Oriental rugs and mahogany furniture. We'd put roses in crystal vases. We'd polish everything with lemon oil. We'd buy yellow songbirds and bamboo cages. There would be enough guestrooms; finally, we'd be the kind of hosts we've always wanted to be. There would be feather mattresses and thick towels. Our guests would feel happy, like cats in velvet laps. The kitchen would be orderly, its canisters of flour and sugar always full. At daybreak, the house would smell like coffee; at night, like steak and peppercorn. Proudly, our mothers would visit. We'd preside calmly over our guests, stirring tea with silver teaspoons. Yes, the highway would still abut the house, but it would be a testament to our powers as homemakers, as magicians, that once inside no guest would recall the anxious city. The cars would waver like dreams beyond the sheer curtains.

But we're poor, and stupid, and blind to the demolition notices. We're the kind of people who press our noses against the glass in museums containing dioramas of old-fashioned houses. Remember those carved wooden creatures we saw in one such museum? They were made for a child long ago, many pairs of animals marching around the nursery and into a toy ark—we would've put them in this house, lined up across the mantelpiece, walking slowly to safety.

mistake #5

Because I'm told that in order to find him one must walk the entire way, I leave the city in August. I walk northward alongside freeways. Trucks honk desperately; I nearly die. Throughout the autumn, I walk. There are orchards, farmhouses, sunsets like cream. The nights grow short. Snow falls. Thankfully my parents raised me for hardship; I know to wear four pairs of socks, and am accustomed to snowflakes grazing my eyeballs. Still, it's not easy.

Eventually I reach the North Pole. Seventeen factories release black smog. There are no wooden signs nailed, sweetly off-kilter, to pine trees. There's no cheerful blizzard, no log cabin, no fireplace, no copper teakettle, no mistletoe, no gingersnaps. It's enough to make one cry, and I do, standing there in that vast treeless expanse.

He's in the sixteenth factory, sitting on a plastic stool. His black hair comes to a violent point above his narrow eyes. He's skinny, slouchy, indifferent, like any factory foreman. He doesn't wear red. He drinks black coffee. His eyes don't widen at the sight of me.

Then—through a doorway—comes a woman who does not disappoint! She wears wooden shoes, long striped socks, green petticoats. She smells of cookies. Her cheeks resemble apples. She looks like the happiest wife in the world. I love her, and want to be her; indeed, I've come to request that exact kind of goodness. She stands before him, radiant. "For Chrissake, Clarissa," he says, "take off that stupid costume." Shivering, she flees.

"The gift . . . I want . . . , " I begin, terrified, "is . . . intangible . . . I was told . . . intangibles . . . could only be requested by people . . . who'd walked. . . ."

"You poor fucking idiot," he says; it's possible that compassion flashes through his eyes.

"Where's the bathroom?" I say wearily. He gestures with his thumb. In the cold dirty stall, I find a long striped sock. I tie it around my neck, lose hope, and head south.

the brides

bride #1

On March 19, 1949, from his Army post at Camp McGill in Japan, my grandfather wrote to my grandmother's father in Asheville, North Carolina: "Perhaps the fact that she and I have spent so much time together has led us to believe that we are in love, whereas we have merely afforded one another much-needed companionship in a strange country and have mistaken our feelings. I really cannot say that we haven't made that mistake."

A pair of porcelain Japanese dolls sank into my grandparents' cake. No one traveled halfway around the globe for the wedding. The photographer accidentally destroyed the film and only one picture remains. This picture could be an advertisement for skin cream. They look so young and so flawless. Filled with hope and fear.

Now, fifty-eight years later, my grandmother's wedding dress hangs on a rod in the middle of our apartment. At times, it's an angel, hovering seven feet off the ground. Other times, it's a ghost and frightens us. Yesterday, we fought: he thought I should put the dress away before the guests arrived; I said there was no room in the closet for such a precious thing, and why would we want to bury my grandmother—you mean your grandmother's dress—away? Though all along I agreed with him.

My grandfather wrote: "Letters to someone who is more or less a stranger always seem to be difficult, especially letters that are particularly important. I'm afraid this will be such a letter."

I remember my grandfather telling my grandmother to put the ice cream away. I remember him ordering many martinis. I remember once overhearing him say he loved her.

Soon, I will marry someone who says that life is a series of intersecting lines, that there is an infinite number of possible intersections, that we have arrived at one such intersection and that it is, all things considered, not such a bad intersection. In fact, quite a good intersection.

That dress, he says, is a phantom point at the place where two lines intersect.

bride #2

In this version of the story, the bride wishes to disappear into the faux groves at the plant nursery. Someone has had the idea of placing two slender white-barked trees on either side of the altar so it will look as though the ceremony is taking place in a delicate forest. Perhaps it was her idea. But now, hearing the others discuss it with the plant nursery employee, she finds it offensively stupid. The bride walks away, toward the trees with their roots aboveground and wrapped in white plastic; white fabric will swath her head twenty-four hours from now. She strolls among the rows. Her heart cries out like a drowning fish. She hears them yelling in the distance, but chooses to attribute the mournful repetitions of her name to the trees themselves.

The rows end at the beach. She steps out onto gray sand where gray waves hit again and again. A chubby mermaid sits on the beach, her tail as pungent as fish-skin in a trashcan. Her hair is the color of pennies and she uses a rock to draw cryptic symbols in the sand, diamonds inside circles. . . . Getting weak coffee in a fishy little seaside café this morning with her parents and future in-laws, everyone talking, making plans, the bride noticed on the wall above them a bad painting of a mermaid drawing cryptic symbols in the sand, the mermaid's arms thick and awkward . . . The bride discovers that the mermaid has vanished from the beach, along with the cryptic symbols. Her heart cries out like a drowning fish.

There are whales in these waters, whales with hearts the size of cars and heartbeats loud enough to be heard two miles away. Naked in the gray water, the bride goes under and listens for whale heartbeats. They find her there. They give her tea, put her to bed, swath her in white, place lilies in her hand, and send her down the aisle toward an altar framed by two slender white-barked trees.

bride #3

I decide that I should like to be married in a straw hat, a straw hat so huge it verges on the ridiculous, and a long red dress with scenes of Japanese tea gardens printed all over it in white, and a pair of large green hoop earrings, and a pair of rhinestone shoes bought on the beach in Los Angeles, and enormous sunglasses with rims the color of Coca-Cola.

I'm sorry, but this is simply what I want to wear when I get married. I refuse to wear anything else. So: I must go out and find these items. But not a single store in New York City has a straw hat as huge as the straw hat in my imagination. Why, why, why, does this always happen? Reality lags so very far behind everything else.

A long red dress with scenes of Japanese tea gardens printed all over it in white? No such luck. There aren't any hoop earrings in the particular grassy shade of green I envision. I live 2,793 miles away from the beach in Los Angeles where they sell rhinestone shoes. And, of course, no sunglasses are as much like Coca-Cola as the sunglasses I desire.

Exhausted from marching around in the obscene murky heat of June, from visiting every single store in New York City, from the music these stores play to manipulate the unmanipulatable imaginations of patrons such as myself, I go back to the miniature cottage where he and I live. The rooms smell of rosemary cooking in olive oil. He is nowhere to be seen. Laid out on the bed is a straw hat; a long red dress; a pair of hoop earrings; a pair of rhinestone shoes; a pair of sunglasses. A confession: none of these objects is quite perfect, none of them aligns flawlessly with the picture in my head—yet suddenly my imagination reshapes itself around these new objects, the objects he has gathered, and now these objects are precisely what I have been thinking of all along.

bride #4

Charlie Chaplin loves me because I throw bananas to the poor, and because I roller-skate backwards. He thinks I have the kind of beauty that will appeal to people of the future; in 100 years, they'll cherish my photograph.

I think he's a small man, and ridiculous. Still, I follow him. We leave New York walking. 'Penguin,' I call him in Harlem. But, obviously, he doesn't say anything. The sun transforms the sidewalk into a desert. Eventually we come to a real desert, and then to another city.

We lie down on the suburban grass. We imagine a home with flowered wallpaper and a cow sticking its head over the geraniums, eager to deliver cream straight into our porridge.

But in fact we live alongside a shallow lake filled with tadpoles. If you slam the front door, the back door topples. Spiders and shingles fall onto the table during dinner. It's difficult to eat with one fork between us. He tries to make the best of things; playfully, he dives into the lake. He gets a concussion and emerges covered with leeches.

I leave and get a job as a dancing girl. He finds me at Mel's and I convince Mel to hire him. I didn't mean to leave Charlie Chaplin, after all, it's just that I fear spiders. He doesn't know how to wait on people, so I pull him onto the dance floor partway through my routine. Unexpectedly, he whistles a French song and dances like an accomplished penguin. Suddenly I love him and want to be his girl.

When the police come for us, we run, though we can't recall our crime. We run until his tuxedo is in rags and a piece of tumbleweed makes off with my dress. I sit on the sand of Nevada to cry for hours. He stands there blocking the sun and, silently, coaxes me out of it.

I stand. Charlie Chaplin takes my hand. We walk down the red road like two old people. There's nothing up ahead, just nothing.

the mothers

mother #1

We the daughters of the twenty-first century are not mystified by Persephone's behavior. In school, we learn that Persephone is frolicking in a field when Hades kidnaps her and takes her underground. Persephone's mother Demeter, the goddess of the harvest, freaks out. Every plant in the world dies. Eventually Persephone is found, sitting beside Hades on an obsidian throne. He's drinking something from a wooden goblet. She looks anorexic. Hades says she can leave if she must but first why doesn't she eat this.

It's not till she emerges into the weird sunlight—it's not till she's in her mother's kitchen sipping pumpkin soup—it's not till Demeter sighs with relief to know her daughter didn't eat anything down there—that Persephone makes her confession about the six pomegranate seeds. Her mother smashes plates, slams doors. Meanwhile, Persephone sits, quietly disliking the freshness of the day, the soft winds carrying the smells of plants growing.

What Persephone will never mention is the rich unending night, the earthy smell of scotch on his breath, the way he mocked the universe and everyone in it but was so tender with the dead, with her, with beasts and ghosts. How low his voice got when he told her attempts would be made to separate them.

Now we the daughters of the twenty-first century are going to marry men our mothers don't quite love. These men seem dark to them, dangerous, lacking in good posture. We sit at our mothers' tables, trying to explain why we have chosen to settle in distant, inhospitable cities where the gray days outnumber the sunny. We try to explain that our future husbands are at once cynical and compassionate. We fight bitterly over wedding invitations and veils, as though these are matters of life and death, which they are. We suggest to our mothers that they read a certain Greek myth; they raise their eyebrows at us as they always do nowadays; the grass begins to shrivel in the ground, and in the orchard the apples sicken on the branch.

mother #2

The bride, the groom, the groom's mother, and the
mother of the bride find themselves at the old carousel. There is no long line of children shrieking out
their cravings and frustrations. The empty evening
carousel whirls to the melancholy sound of its own
cheerful music. The groom's mother, a woman who
has made her share of rhubarb pies, suggests they take
a ride. The mother of the bride, who resists silliness,
hangs back; but already the groom has bought tickets,
and here they are stepping onto the carousel, and the
bride straddles a black horse, and the groom selects
a chestnut, and the groom's mother finds a pony, and
the mother of the bride must mount the unicorn. The
bride looks at ease, as though she is still a child, and
still capable of delight. She strokes the horse's frightening glass eyes; she discovers that the mane is real
horsehair; she has no difficulty being happy; she hisses
something delightful to the groom. The mother of the

bride finds it awkward, adults sitting on these creatures built for children. None of this is right, none of it at all. Slowly, the carousel begins. The mother of the bride recalls something: the bride, age four, clinging to the pole of a carousel, a frozen white stallion rearing under her. But now this carousel accelerates, and the ocean breeze blows in, and the mother of the bride stops thinking about anything except the brass ring, reaching out again and again with her half-century arm—all is well! All is well! The carousel whirls, life is a joyful and colorful endeavor, it is not impossible to achieve the sensation of flight, bless these young people and bless their mothers, all's well, and where's that blessed brass ring because the mother of the bride is starting to believe. Jubilation, the bride has been saying lately, and the bride's use of this word has irritated her mother; now she wants to say Jubilation too.

But it is not she who gets the brass ring.

mother #3

My mother, during any conversation about a sad or complicated situation, sighs and says, "Well, that's just the nature of the beast." It's impossible for the discussion to progress beyond this point; her pronouncement always silences me.

However, I should like to know more about this beast! What is it, and what exactly is its nature? Based on context, I can tell the beast has terrible luck, is continually embroiled in conflict, doesn't appreciate what it's been given, forgets to have its oil changed, gets pregnant too frequently, and generally blunders through life. Poor beast!

The beast is three times the size of a regular sow. Thick hairs grow out of her thick hide. She has many sagging nipples. Two offspring clamor for each. She has six legs and an enormous, friendly rhinoceros head. Her teeth are yellow and sharp, but her lips are tender. She shuffles them along the spines of her babies. Her hooves are delicate; upon them she moves in a stately manner down sidewalks and through woods.

She walks back and forth across this great nation, hoping that someday we'll understand her nature. At night, she and her children lie down in public parks or behind barns where, in a better world, they might be cared for by a farmer with no fear of beasts. The beast never shuts her moon-colored eyes. Her nature is tranquil, strong, maternal, and benevolent.

I don't know how to tell my mother the truth about the nature of the beast. I fear what might happen if she were not able to attribute so many problems to it.

My mother and I are driving on a superhighway at dusk. Someone we know has done something awful and irrational. My mother explains that this is the nature of the beast. In the fading Western light, sunset orange and gray over mountains, dying daylight versus manmade floodlights, I spot the beast trotting along in the shoulder. Her children cling to her belly and back. But the wonderful beast—she just keeps trotting and trotting.

mother #4

In this version, I like my mother and my mother likes me. We walk together, her arm around my waist and mine around hers, and she is not embarrassed; we walk together, leaving the city. My mother is no longer brittle and no longer skinny; she reminds me of a buttery corn muffin, the likes of which you never would have found in the bran-infested kitchen of my childhood. "Don't drink orange juice," my mother said back then. "It's an empty drink." I didn't understand, and I didn't drink orange juice.

My mother who is no longer brittle leads me into a field. Thousands of miniature orange flowers grow in this field. Our eyes are no longer bloodshot. My mother sighs with joy. She sits. She instructs me to place my head in her lap. All my headaches vanish. "Never call me Mother," she says. "Only call me Momma, or some other nice thing."

This mother of mine has things to tell me about

marriage. I say "Oh!" to everything she says because everything is a revelation. She bestows upon me certain facts that bear repeating, such as: *On the wedding day, you must adorn your bare head with waxy white yucca blossoms so the rain won't melt you and your husband,* and *There is no fight that cannot be resolved by boiling cloves and orange peels in water on the stove.*

She says to me, "What a beautiful fat girl you are, my daughter." I say: "I am not fat. Look at this skinny hip." She says: "Darling child, what I mean to say is that you are fat with life."

And then I notice that all this time her fingers have been working, and she has woven me a garment from the miniature orange flowers, and caterpillars are crawling all over this garment, and my fat wise mother is laughing, laughing, and she is laughing, and she is saying, "Where is the groom, where is the beautiful fat groom, ah my daughter is ready, my daughter is ready!"

mother #5

Before my mother comes to visit, I become a warrior, tracking down every molecule of imperfection in my apartment and doing away with it. I find and destroy invisible crumbs, dust, mildew, mold. I sweep. I vacuum. I mop places that don't need mopping. I bend my back. I get down on my knees. I scrub until my wrists ache. I fill my vases with orchids I can't afford; I fill the refrigerator with imported grapes and mineral water.

When I was young, this is how my mother prepared for her mother. Once, as a teenager, I screamed over the roar of the vacuum: *Won't your mother be overjoyed to see you whether or not the rugs have been vacuumed?* My mother grinned strangely—as I grin now, wiping nonexistent cobwebs from baseboards—and said something that could not be heard. Later, I said: *When I am grown I will not do this for you when you come to visit.* And she said: *Yes you will.*

And I do.

In the house where I grew up, there is a grand old mahogany clock on the mantelpiece. My mother adores this clock, which came from her mother. I always hated it; I couldn't stand the way it pompously counted out each second, delivering me closer to death with every tock.

When my mother comes to visit, she gives me a clock. A square clock with a round face. Silver, black, and modern, it makes almost no noise at all. It is a splendid object. My mother frets over this clock, which seems to have neglected to mark the four hours it spent airborne. She flips it over and examines the bowels of it. She twists certain knobs; and suddenly the clock reports the proper time. I wish it told the wrong time, four hours early or sixteen minutes late, or it could just sit there with its hands unmoving and I'd love it even more.

In any case: my mother has brought me a clock, and we are overjoyed to see each other.

the weddings

wedding #1

This is not story-telling, this is record-keeping: on June 21, 2007, HCP and ADT were married in Manhattan's City Hall at 1:28 p.m. The one-minute-seventeen-second ceremony was witnessed by LMH and performed by a court clerk in a pink tracksuit by the name of JT. HCP carried a bouquet of one yellow, three red, two orange, and two pink Gerber daisies, wrapped with white ribbon by a sympathetic woman in a flower shop. There was a bureaucratic window with the word CHAPEL printed over it. HCP, ADT, and LMH waited in line for a long time before they were called. JT said will you love, honor, cherish, etc., and HCP and ADT said they would. LMH bought them lunch at a restaurant in Chinatown with images of bamboo forests and waterfalls on the walls. Afterward the newlyweds bought a cheap turtle carved from unprecious stone. Old ladies on the street said where did you get those splendid flowers and HCP said I am married now, I am married.

In Washington Square Park the sun was too brilliant, the fountain sprayed too high, everyone got wet, too wet, too bright, there were sunburns, kids played nearly naked.

They looked up at thousands of leaves and ADT said: As many leaves as are there, that's probably about how many hours we'll spend together. HCP said: Or is it as many minutes as we'll spend together? It's hard to do the math. Then they ate cupcakes, or maybe the cupcakes were beforehand, but it was all green and sweet and bright and the events get confused in one's mind.

LMH left, and in a French café HCP and ADT drank white wine. When they asked the dear waitress for the bill, she informed them that the man at table 14 paid it; the man at table 14 had already left, and they'd never noticed him.

On the longest day of 2007, someone stalked a unicorn. The water beneath the Brooklyn Bridge turned to wine. This is not record-keeping; this is storytelling.

wedding #2

When my grandfather's second wife died at the age of 93, he couldn't put her away. She'd been so happy with him! She, a virgin when she married him at 90! He kept her there, sitting at the table in her blue silk suit. It was touching, and terrible. Meanwhile, he entertained old ladies in the parlor. Once, she moved her thumb slightly as my guy and I passed by. "Excuse me," I said, "but aren't you dead?" The funeral director's makeup did wonders; still, it wasn't pleasant. "Are you mad about the old ladies?" I said. An imperceptible nod.

The next day, we visited my grandfather at his bead store. Whores riffled through sequins. My grandfather was kind, suggesting rhinestones to match their eyes. That place was a treasure box. We could have stayed forever, running our fingers through barrels of beads. But we had business to attend to. Knowing how Grandpa hated grammatical incorrectness, I said: "Your old lady don't like the new old ladies. She's dead but that don't mean she don't know!"

He said, "'Doesn't,' child."

"Grandpa, you're breaking her poor old broke-down heart!"

"Child, you don't know nothin' about nothin'.'"

It was frightening when he talked wrong. It meant he meant what he said. My guy and I looked at each other and announced: "We swear we'll never do to each other what Grandpa's doing to her. If you or I die, I won't entertain ladies or men. I'll notice when you move your thumb. This we swear, so help us."

My grandfather smiled. He told us to go where the skyscrapers end. Told us about a rock there by the ocean. Said we'd find a "T" written in chalk. Said we should stand on either side, should look out at the ocean, should say some words, and then would be married. We did as he instructed; there, on that rock, one could forget the whole damn city. The wilderness of the ocean overcame us, stretching out and away like a metaphor for something.

wedding #3

I think of the letters that compose the syllables that compose your names: the A's! the B's! the C's! the D's! the E's! the F's! the G's! the H's! the I's! the J's! the K's! the L's! the M's! the N's! the O's! the P's! the Q's! the R's! the S's! the T's! the U's! the V's! the W's! the X's! the Y's! the Z's! Dear wedding guests: I think of you in planes and buses, in cars and trains, on fast ferries and slow, smiling or not smiling, your eyes open or not open; however ancestral you may be, today you seem to me like the sleepy children I'll someday bear. I believe you'll find the rosehips on this island larger and more monstrous than any you have ever seen; I believe you'll find the spiderwebs shinier and more alluring. Forgive the bride and groom if they giggle at the altar; they are giggling for grief, just as you are crying for joy. Everything is chaos. Down by the sea, you'll discover a small man and a small woman living in a small house, and they are happy. Oh—did we forget to mention?—the water served at our wedding—it's stolen water—it will make you immortal for the time being—and perhaps for much longer—Drink! Your head should be spinning and spinning. You should have forgotten your own name by now. This is it!—the party of which I always dreamed so desperately. I thought only flood or fire would bring us together—but here we are. Your faces should be dripping with sweat. Your skirts should be pulled up high to reveal your fat or skinny legs beneath. Your buttons should be popping off your shirts. When I come round to dance with you, you should make me dizzy. (If/When) I die, I shall be glad to have been near you for these few hours; I shall be glad to have had the letters of your wonderful, fragile names swirling around in my brain. Goodbye, dear ghosts! Hello, dear ghosts!

wedding #4

I swear to you: we were all there! Light from lanterns made of colored paper fell across our faces as darkness came. Listen: we all sat on the front porch, those of us too young to walk in the laps of those of us too old to walk. There were three guitars and twelve men who could play guitar, and one boy who remembered the melodies and another boy who remembered the lyrics. There were girls with large green joyous earrings, and girls whose skirts kept getting lifted by the breeze, and girls with gleaming hair. There were men with large red joyous faces, and men drinking wine, and men drinking beer. Oh! It was too much, I'm telling you, too much: our bodies are not capable of containing such happiness. Family-and-friends. There was no rain. There was no threat of flood. The candles did not get out of hand; no fire raged. For a matter of hours, it was as though we all lived in a village with cobblestone streets. It was as though my mother was the town baker, and my father was the lamplighter, and my cousin was the fishmonger, and my sister sold peaches, and my friends sold flowers, and my uncle built doors. It was as though we all owned small houses and grew lavender in our window boxes. It was as though we all had porches with rocking chairs and honeysuckle. The aeroplane had not yet been invented, nor the steam engine, nor the automobile. Our clocks had to be wound by hand and were always inaccurate. We measured time by the slow ripening of the grapes in our arbors. Our cradles were made of pine; our wheelbarrows were heavy with tomatoes; our brides wore daisies around their heads; our church needed no decoration beyond sunbeams; our grooms weren't nervous. We were all there, I swear we were! I swear that for a matter of hours the world was the way it ought to be; and I refuse to mention what happened next.

wedding #5

Something is happening at the altar: first, the bride's veil begins to tremble, and the groom buries his chin in his bowtie. Her veil trembles until it's downright shaking. He buries his chin deeper into his bowtie. His face has become as red as her bouquet; weak-kneed, she reaches out to support herself against his tuxedoed chest, though the ceremony has not yet arrived at the moment when it's appropriate for her to touch him. The wedding guests shift uneasily in the pews. Everything was fine, everything was normal, until the priest asked the bride to make her most solemn vow—and now, this! This odd, even rude, behavior, the shaking of the veil and the burying of the chin and the reddening of the face and the reaching for the chest, all of which is now accompanied by a—sound! A rather recognizable sound . . . can it—can it be? Are these two young people—this handsome groom, this beautiful bride—are they—are they—*giggling* at the altar?

Indeed they are! Giggling like kids hiding under a

blanket in the basement during a thunderstorm! The bride so overwhelmed by peals of laughter that she's incapable of answering the question put her by the priest! Right before their very eyes, the guests watch this shameful laughter evolve into guffaws. The bride drops her bouquet. The ring tumbles unnoticed from the groom's palm. The bride leans forward in a most unladylike position, slapping her thigh through layers of satin. The groom leans backward, throwing his chin up toward the cross where Christ hangs. A button pops off his starched shirt and hits her square on the nose, which sends them—can you imagine?—even further into their glee.

One of the guests decides to leave, and then another, and another, tiptoeing down the aisle, all of them slowly fleeing, passing through the doors with barely controlled indignation, followed soon by the priest, everyone abandoning the so-called bride and the so-called groom there at the altar, where they howl with laughter, dissolve into laughter.

wedding #6

Because the wedding was a failure, rows upon rows of empty pews filling the cathedral, we headed into the wilderness. We were certain that somewhere in this vast green country we'd find someone willing to serve as witness to our marriage. At night, we snuck through suburbs, darting between manicured bushes beneath orange streetlights. Finally we reached the endless green meadows of which we'd heard rumors. Not yet man and wife, we held hands like Adam and Eve as we walked through the thick miraculous grass, breathless with awe; for once, reality exceeded our imaginations.

Then. We saw them. There were two of them. They were enormous. They were like the elephants in the zoo times ten. They were covered in fur. They had long tusks and mean black eyes. They were far grander and more dangerous than anything we'd ever seen. Peacefully, they grazed in the meadows. They plucked the grass with their incredible trunks. We could hear the rhythm of their jaws as they chewed.

This is a true story! It is not a story from any era but our own! In the infinite green meadows of America, we hid behind a small boulder. But unfortunately, that small boulder turned out to be the infant of the beasts. The infant stirred as we leaned against it, and the parents rushed toward us, trumpeting with a sound that was like all the orchestras in the world playing one note at the same time. The infant mewled; the parents trumpeted. With the odd calm that arises from inevitability, we prepared to die. Each of them grabbed one of us in its trunk, each coiled and squeezed; later, comparing notes, we would agree that their fur smelled simultaneously of lavender and snot. We were tossed several miles, back into the suburbs, where we landed on two adjacent lawns in the broad light of day; housewives emerged at doorways to see what horror was disrupting the perfection of the afternoon; we came toward each other, and realized that now we were married.

the wives

wife #1

Today being married to you makes my heart feel like a cucumber, long and cold and awkwardly shaped for the cavity in which it belongs. The new brides are not interested in my advice. They tell me to buzz off. Their nails are encrusted with diamonds that will be thrown away at the end of the day. If I knew where they'd be washing their hands, I'd follow them and gather those diamonds. They're tiny, indeed, and yellowish in color, but nonetheless.

Because I am so difficult, we go to a motel. *In the motel, there you feel free.* Yet I and my cucumber fail you again. We leave at 5:17 a.m. after a few hours of terrifying sleep, during which your limbs strewn over me felt like a hot, fleshy web. (In the past, your arms and legs always served as a shield of blood and bone, defending me from nightmares.) I gasped, got thirsty. My eyes so dry they felt like knives.

The streets are murky. You could have picked a

different bride. Yet here we are, burdened with luggage, limping, and I am insisting that I need a notebook, a pencil, a table, in order to record phrases such as "Today being married to you makes my heart feel like X."

At sunup, we find ourselves alongside a wide black river where a boat bearing a bridal party moves eastward, gleaming. You take me to an old library with a heavy wooden desk. The ghost of our future daughter runs naughtily down the stone hallway. You chase her, feeding her bits of banana. I try to write: "during which your limbs strewn over me felt like X X, X X." But I cannot recall! "My X so X they felt like X." I'd had something to say about the sound of many doors slamming. I'd wanted to attack you with sharp questions. I'd wanted to know precisely why you hadn't selected one of the other, better brides. Our nonexistent daughter! She's so noisy, playing hide-and-go-seek with you.

wife #2

The men who killed unicorns were men no different from us. Some of them had narrow, lazy eyes with which they looked back toward the castle where the nude queen was just now pulling open her curtains; some of them had wide, stupid faces and oversized thumbs and awaited bloodshed; some of them were intelligent, and enjoyed making pronouncements with their index fingers pointed upward. The men who killed unicorns—they too had trouble waking in the morning. They too got tired of their wives. They too masturbated in the dark as teenagers. Their anatomical hearts functioned just as ours do. Like us, they were uncomfortable walking through the forest, sometimes hot and sometimes cold, sometimes scratched by thorns and sometimes sinking in mud. Like us, they had trouble believing in the existence of unicorns. And yet they proceeded, crushing thousands of flowers.

Some facts about unicorns: (1) If a unicorn does not wish hunters to find him, they will not find him.

(2) The eyes of a unicorn are identical to the eyes of a human being. (3) Unicorns are wilder and crueler than anyone would have imagined. (4) Unicorns can impale three dogs at once on their horns. (5) Unicorns mate for life.

Listen: A peasant girl comes upon a unicorn drinking at the brook. Startled, he impales her on his horn. The town witch heals her. The peasant girl can't help but go looking for the unicorn. A bluebird takes flight above the fruits of the forest. The unicorn follows her home. She builds a fence around him. There are many droplets of red on his white back. Do not mistake them for blood! They are the juice of pomegranate seeds fallen from the pomegranate tree above his enclosure. Happily married, the unicorn and the girl sleep entwined like one strange creature. She clenches her toes, squeezing his haunch. In captivity, the unicorn smiles.

In other words: I am sorry, young husband, for the mistakes I made last week. Our ancestors were unicorn-hunters, and so are we.

wife #3

Bob Dylan is happy today, thank God! He says he likes October in Brooklyn. Astonishingly, he shows up at our place before noon. He's wearing those tight black jeans that make his legs look like crows, but get this—he asks to borrow my husband's most cheerful winter sweater. My husband has things to do and can't join us. Bob Dylan stares and glares as we peck goodbye in the doorway.

In the park, Bob Dylan wants to watch the swans. They're regal, bitchy swans. He says swans are descended from snakes; he says their long, creepy necks prove it. The swans glide like queens and narrow their eyes at us. He's in such a good mood! He lifts his sunglasses and asks questions about the pregnancy, even reaches over to touch my stomach. It's never like this when we see each other. Usually he stalks along silent at my side, grimly remembering the seven nicknames he once had for me.

At the farmers' market, Bob Dylan helps me choose

apples, though he's not careful about avoiding those that are less than firm. After exchanging the ones he threw into the bag, I turn around to discover a crowd of kids gathered around him, watching him juggle apples. Because of the reindeer sweater, no one recognizes him; Bob Dylan would never wear such a garment.

On the way home I carry apples, bread, yogurt, honey, eggs, squash, onions. Bob Dylan doesn't offer to help. He's not the type to notice when a pregnant woman is overburdened. He didn't make it to our wedding, and now he asks about it. I don't know what to tell him. I tell him I wore a crown of small daisies. "Of course you did!" he says joyously, if I dare use that word in conjunction with him. What I don't mention is the night a month after the wedding when I stayed up secretly with the old tapes, listened to him sing about all the vanished girls, began to wonder if I was already dead.

wife #4

We owe so much to the brave woman who first cut into an onion and went through with the gesture! I don't know in what era of human history this occurred—certainly hundreds, if not thousands, of eager homemakers had attempted and (weeping) failed to chop an onion before our heroine emerged. It was she who could ignore her instinct screaming out that any food capable of making a human cry was not a food a human ought to eat. It was she who could ignore the implication, based on her tears, that the onion would be disgusting at best, poisonous at worst.

I imagine her in a kitchen, though surely this happened before the time of kitchens. Let's make it a primitive kitchen then, counters carved in a stone cave and water dripping down walls. Let's say she's gone out into the wilderness and dug up one perfect onion. Let's say she's brought it home with pride and conviction. She peels away papery layers. With her crude knife, she cuts into it. For a moment, all's well. She notices the milky juice of it on her fingers. She smells it, and finds it a great, rich fragrance. It reminds her of the way he smells down there. But then: the tears come. Though she's seen others cry, she has never cried herself. She's bewildered, disconcerted—until she decides that she cannot be responsible for this impossible situation, tears in her brave, cold eyes; it must be that roguish onion. And she attacks.

That night, he stares worshipfully at her while devouring piece after piece of onion. Neighbors come from all around; they fill with envy and admiration when they taste onion for the first time. The men regret that they didn't select this woman; the women dip their heads in shame.

I too am jealous of her, she who could separate one kind of crying from another. Even knowing all I know, still whenever he comes home and asks why I'm crying I can't say *Oh it's just the onions.*

wife #5

It started out fine. Delightful, even. One of us (later we couldn't recall which) bought a pair of little brown birds. Our imitation of a happy marriage was still impeccable at that point; we ourselves did not realize it was an imitation. The birds had reminded the purchaser of a sight we'd seen in Latin America: an unfinished cathedral, wrecked by an earthquake partway through construction. It looked almost intentional, those jagged half-walls giving way to the terribly blue sky where the dome would have been, as though this was the best way to approach God. Weeds grew among the disintegrating bricks, sporting flowers of a brilliant pink hue that, in our country, can be found only on candy wrappers. Birds darted across the non-existent dome. Yes, that memory somehow resonated with the sight of these birds in their pet-shop carrying case, and we went out to buy a cage.

Two birds wasn't enough, we decided, for two, as we knew, could get lonely. And once you had three, their tittering interfering with all your thoughts anyhow, the strange yet innocuous smell of their shit filling the apartment, why not four? Why not eight? Why not a whole flock? We named them, though it was impossible to keep them straight. We took pictures of them. Our co-workers called us the Bird People; we enjoyed the title.

But we hadn't prepared ourselves for death. When the first one went, we were shocked, speechless, staring at the tiny carcass. Then one of us convinced the other that someday we'd own a yard where we could bury it. In the meantime? We wrapped it in tinfoil and put it in the freezer.

After that, we no longer kept our birds in cages. It seemed the least we could do. Every surface in our apartment bore a thin gloss of bird shit. We watched TV while the birds dipped and whirred above us. Eventually, our freezer became overfull with bird corpses. Someday, we told each other tensely at night, we'll have a yard.

wife #6

Two friends meet in a café. One is recently and secretly divorced. One is recently and secretly married. They choose to sit in the courtyard behind the café. An uncertain warmth curls around the chilly wind. Spring is arriving. They wish to liberate their bodies from the cold, strange winter. Each has been feeling apocalyptic lately, and brave. By the time they've determined—egging each other on—to sit outside, by the time they've overmastered the waiter's cocked eyebrow and warning about the cold metal chairs, by the time they've gotten settled at the wrought-iron table in the deserted courtyard, they've gone too far to retract their decision, to return to the interior where lamps glow yellow on chocolate walls. Each has come to tell the other her secret. They talk politely, then fall silent.

One of the women stares into her white mug. She taps her cold feet on the flagstone. She glances at her friend and looks away. She grips the mug. She stares at the barren branches. She notices birdsong; is her attention to such details heightened due to the recent circumstances of her life? She glances at her friend again. She observes certain tiny effects of age in her friend's face. "So," she says.

The other woman glances at her friend and looks away. She stares at the barren branches. She grips her white mug. She glances at her friend again. She observes certain tiny effects of age in her friend's face. She taps her cold feet on the flagstone. She stares into the mug. She notices birdsong; is her attention to such details heightened due to the recent circumstances of her life? "So," she says, just as her friend says, "So."

They talk politely. "So," each sometimes begins, but nothing comes of it. Eventually, they both say they must be going. Shivering, they come in from the courtyard. The waiter grins triumphantly. He was right. They were wrong. The friends part in the vestibule of the café; it will be decades before they see each other again.

wife #7

I am dead now and an old woman who barely speaks English has come to prepare my face for burial. She says "revjuneate" rather than "rejuvenate." The warm damp cloth she rubs across my face calls to mind the warm damp cloth Nana rubbed across my face when I was little. It's too late now to explain that I'd prefer to burn instead, that I've always been curious about the color of the flames my body would release. Someone has decided—I wonder with shock if it's you—that there will be calla lilies, a coffin, a line of people, a cemetery, a terrible clump of dirt. The old woman massages my cheeks with rose-scented cream. I wish this had happened to me more frequently when I was alive. I can tell from the tenderness in her fingertips that she finds me quite beautiful. This calls to mind the statue of Mary in the churchyard—mournfully hopeful, her loving white fingertips turned upward.

It's too late now to tell you about a little girl

bouncing an enormous white ball on the roof of a sky-scraper. I wanted to describe to you the rubbery sound it made, the thrilling and ominous sensation in the stomach as it reached its apex, the belief that if the ball bounced off the side perhaps I'd become capable of flight. It was a blindingly white ball. She bounced it hundreds of times.

The old woman has revjuneated me as best she can. She has applied powders everywhere, and something moist to the lips. I died young, kind of, but not tragically young. She turns off the light, kisses my forehead. I wonder if I'm not little again, asleep in Nana's house.

It's too late now to tell you that when the little girl bounced the ball to me, I bounced it back to her. We became involved in a game that we both took very seriously. I was not pregnant when I died, not exactly, but soon I would have been. It would've been a little girl.

wife #8

Once you've been dead for a period of time, you know how true it is that we each die alone; and indeed Snow White remained vaguely cognizant of this truth even after her life had revived and resolved itself in joyous ways. . . .

She and Prince X were a happy couple. (In fact, everyone found them infuriatingly darling, and whenever they were paraded through the streets the roses tossed upon them contained, tucked among their petals, small cryptic curses—*Sixteen onions in a barrel of brine, You may be hers but she is mine!* Of course the royal couple never saw these; only the hunchbacked, dwarfish street-sweepers read them, giggling strangely.) They were happy . . . but Prince X was a dreamy fellow and sometimes vanished into his imagination, leaving her alone with her knowledge that we each die alone. She searched for him in dusty abandoned towers. Speculating that perhaps he had been magically shrunken, she hunted for him in the sugar bowl.

By the time he reappeared, barging through the bronze doors and proposing a picnic on the parapet, she'd already become lost in solitude. She wondered if the huntsman had removed her heart and replaced it with a clump of frozen dirt. What else could explain this coldness in her, this immunity to his eager eyes? How she wished she could coo back at him! But we each die alone! "Polgi nitsway," she said apologetically. "Ogblitefa?"

"What a joker you are!" he exclaimed, embracing her.

"Ikne faldig ti!" She squirmed away and ran to the mirror. She was herself—black hair! pure skin! red lips!—and yet she was not. "Folea badong, u lemrig!" It was no joke—this had become the only language she knew. Her solitude swelled and completed itself. For days she would live lonesomely at his side, her heart like a tin can and her mouth producing unrecognizable words.

Eventually, her mind would wrap itself around his language again. Again she would be darling enough to parade under showers of roses, happy enough to forget the truth.

wife #9

Once upon a time, a happy young wife set out to visit her family. In the months since their union, the couple had established the minor rituals of marriage: certain patterns of holding and shifting during sleep. He stood in the doorway. He placed a finger against the pulse in her neck. He knew she'd soon return.

At the farm, nobody mentioned the hateful words that had been exchanged when she ran off to be married. Instead, they gave her a cup of milk. They stroked her hair. Later, they laid her in her childhood bed. She helped in the orchard. On the sixth day, approaching the farmhouse on the familiar path, she wondered briefly if perhaps she'd only imagined her husband, if she'd made him up while strolling down this very path.

After two weeks, the husband—who'd been awaiting her return for over a week—appeared in the yard. He observed that, oddly, she looked somewhat younger than before—her skin, perhaps, a shade more radiant.

She held a pail. She pretended not to recognize him. How dear and playful she was! But the game went on too long; she screamed when he reached for her, and ran inside. Torn between bemusement and terror, he plunked down under a pear tree. The family looked out the window at him. "Who *is* that fellow?" the young wife asked them.

At night she sucked her thumb, as he learned when he spied into her bedroom. It saddened him that he hadn't known this fact. She was smaller than he remembered. He sat under the pear tree, watching her. Eventually her sisters brought him water, but she shuddered whenever she passed by. He sat there for a long time, becoming skeletal and unshaven. The family put up with him. She avoided him. Yet he observed that she was getting younger each day. By the time she was a toddler, she'd approach him on unsteady legs and yank his spectacular beard. When she became an infant, he rocked her and dripped milk into her mouth.

the offspring

offspring #1

She sees abandoned babies everywhere. A baby sitting on the pavement in a red snowsuit. A baby crawling down the subway platform toward a dead rat. A baby riding a swan across the lake. Her heart does acrobatics as she rushes to rescue them. Instantaneously, she envisions a wooden crib in her apartment, sunbeams illuminating a bottle of warm milk.

But it's just a red fire hydrant. A paper bag blowing down the subway platform toward a candy wrapper. A trick of light on the swan's wings. Sadly, the world is not filled with abandoned babies. She stops running, cringes, turns away.

She cannot stop humming: *hush a bye baby in the treetop when the wind blows the cradle will rock when the bough breaks the cradle will drop down will come baby cradle and all hush a—*

Whenever she passes a big tree, she looks up. Surely someday she'll come upon one with a cradle in its highest branches. She can picture this happening, not in the magical pink light of a lullaby but in the cold honest light of reality—the wind blows, the cradle rocks, the rope slips, the cradle drops. The impact of its fall bruises her chin, but there it is, in her arms, a wooden cradle containing an abandoned baby. She'll change the lyrics to something gentler: *Hush a bye baby in the toyshop, when the frog croaks the monkey will bop.*

She cannot stop humming. She cannot stop seeing abandoned babies everywhere. One time the abandoned baby is not a fire hydrant nor a paper bag nor a swan's wing. It is a real baby, lying on a blanket while its mother chases the dog. It is not necessary to rescue the baby under these circumstances, yet she does. Afterward, they take her somewhere: a pale room. They give her an acorn squash wrapped in a blanket. Sometimes the acorn squash is an abandoned baby. Sometimes it's just an acorn squash. She holds it close, waiting for it to turn back into a baby.

offspring #2

At the Anne Frank School for Expectant Mothers, we're given cream for our tea and permission to pick unlimited peaches from the trees alongside the dormitory. Anne Frank doesn't want anyone to feel deprived. Each day, she instructs us in how to overcome gravity. The meadow is ragged, its grass destroyed by the feet of generations of expectant mothers. The sky is pale, perfect, enticing. First Anne Frank explains the mechanics of flight. Then she tells us we must fill ourselves with ferocious terror and ferocious tenderness; only then will we rise. This she knows from experience. Anne Frank, who is always eight months pregnant but never bears a child, has dark and wonderful eyes. We love her desperately. Her arms are impossibly skinny, yet when she flaps them she begins to rise. Soon she's ten feet above us, fifteen, forty, swooping through the clean morning. We attempt, flopping in the mud like wet chickens. "*Ferocity*," Anne Frank commands. "There will be times," Anne Frank tells us as we trip and sob in the mud, "when there's no alternative but flight." Nervously, we ask her to elaborate, but she falls silent. By nighttime, we're exhausted, earthbound. We just want to sit on the veranda and brush Anne Frank's thick black hair until it glows. We trade off, passing the hairbrush. Knowing how to fly is essential if we're to become the kind of mothers we hope to be. And by the end of the two-week course, several women can, with much puffing and aching, rise six feet. The rest of us are failures. Anne Frank gives us our badges anyhow. She's very forgiving. She watches as we board the bus that will return us to our bemused men. Her eye sockets so deep her eyes look like bruises.

Thirteen years later, when they come for my daughter, I shriek and get ferocious, grab her and try to rise over fire escapes, clotheslines, flagpoles, garbage heaps; but there must be something Anne Frank forgot to tell us about how to achieve flight.

offspring #3

It's disgusting, so I throw it away, but my daughter reaches into the trashcan, pulls it out, puts it on the table, and places her finger on its rotting mottled skin. As her fingertip disappears into the decaying peach, she looks upward, saintly, at the wooden ceiling, the copper pots, the dried herbs rattling in the wind coming from the garden.

"Ugh," I say loudly. "Disgusting."

As she stands there, one hand absorbed by the peach and the other on her belly, I'm suddenly stricken, or rather, *slapped* by the roundness of her: cheeks, chin, breasts, belly, bum.

Slowly the peach becomes firm again. Her finger begins to reemerge from its depths.

I go to the window. From here I can observe the gray day, cars on the highway twenty-three stories below, can remind myself what a vast bleak block this is, can turn back to face her. There's no wooden ceiling here, and there never was. There are no copper pots, no herbs, no wind from the garden; in fact, no garden at all. There's just a kitchen with linoleum floors. There's just a laughable balcony clinging to this massive apartment building, scarcely room for two and certainly not room if one happens to be pregnant.

But there *is* this brown peach turning pink beneath her fingers. There is this young woman who possesses many kinds of roundness; in such roundness copper pots appear, and gardens.

She lifts the now-ripe peach to my nose. Its fragrance gives me a headache.

"How bout that!" I exclaim. "Lemme see." Grinning, gleaming, childlike, she hands it to me. I stroke it—too similar to the skin of an infant. She looks at me with such delight—come *on*, it's just a small miracle, just one salvaged peach—that I become claustrophobic. I rush to the balcony, a journey of one step in this silly apartment, and hurl the peach onto the highway below.

Turning back around, I find that the delight has yet to drain completely from her face. "Mom," she whispers mournfully at me.

offspring #4

Whenever my mother got frustrated by the quality of the lettuce in the supermarket, she'd kick off her shoes and vanish. Accustomed to such behavior, I'd lounge among the potatoes until she reappeared with an armful of lettuce so bright green and dewy it looked like it had been harvested moments before. Her face always seemed pale after these disappearances, but also there was an additional radiance about her. The girls working the checkout never noticed the incredible lettuce. Silently, I wondered why my mother insisted on paying for lettuce that didn't come from the store. "It's important to me and your father that you have the semblance of a normal life," she said. As usual, nothing in my mind was opaque to her.

If we passed a homeless man on the street, she'd kick off her shoes and vanish. Moments later, she'd reappear with a bag of food, a set of clothing in his size, and a winter coat. The exhausted men accepted these things without surprise.

My father kicked off his shoes and vanished if the bus was moving slowly and he was running late. He also kicked off his shoes and vanished whenever he discovered, through mysterious channels, that terrorists had boarded airplanes.

My parents were not particular about their powers; they used them to solve both mundane and catastrophic problems. When, as a thirteen-year-old, I questioned the ethics of this, my father did not allow me to verbalize my doubts before he informed me that all problems are equally small and equally great.

On my sixteenth birthday, I kicked off my shoes and vanished. I was no longer in our kitchen. Instead, I was diving off a cliff above the Pacific Ocean. I could not tell if I was flying or falling. In the waves below, I saw the heads of giraffes sticking up, and the trunks of elephants. The sun was bright and green. I was filled with a strange weighty joy, as though the entire world had been passed on to me for safekeeping.

offspring #5

Once, a boy was given a spool of thread by a beautiful, monstrous woman. When he pulled the thread, time passed very quickly. If the school day was boring, he could pull the thread, and the afternoon would be over. If he got tired of serving in the military, if he couldn't wait until his wedding, if he was eager for the birth of his first son, if he wanted to reach retirement, he could pull the thread; and that is what he did. He lived his life rapidly, skipping from one grand moment to the next. Soon, he was an extremely old man. It was a hot afternoon in the village. He was sick of looking at the same fields, sick of hearing the same laborers yell the same curses to one another, sick of the gruel his granddaughter had placed before him. It would be so much better if evening would come already, bringing with it cold blue light and silence and a basket of plums. He reached for his spool of thread, only to discover that less than half a centimeter remained. So if he were to pull it—! Horrified, the old man began winding the spool he'd spent his whole life unwinding. He wound and wound until he was a boy again, watching a beautiful, monstrous woman disappear into a crowd. This boy took the spool of thread home and hid it in the attic. Many decades later, long after he'd lived his entire life and was dead, someone found the spool and used it to mend something.

This summer is passing quickly, we realize; and yet it sits weightily upon us. The leaves of the trees sweat in the afternoon. At night we can hardly sleep for the heat. Sometimes we become gloomy. Our necks ache from holding our heads up under the humidity. We think of moving to a newer, gentler place; we think of our nonexistent children. Walking past the vast beautiful graveyard, we envision our gravestones, lined up side by side.

offspring #6

Suddenly and against all odds, we had the things we wanted. Our baby had been born and was hot as an oven—you held that child, and warmth suffused you. A burning little machine of life. We finally owned a home: one white-walled room with hardwood floors followed by another and another etc. The highway was just far enough away that the fast cars sounded like the sea. Our first night in our new home, we crossed the threshold bolstered by many blessings, for who doesn't bless two young people, an infant, a new house? We walked through the first room, the second, the third, happiness transforming our hearts into fireworks. A hot little baby at the nipple! Our muscles full of invisible health! The shiny floors reflecting the full moon! Our hearts shooting upwards! No touch of doubt in us anymore!

In the final room, we came upon nine pirates sitting around our dining table. They were all dirty in different ways, missing different body parts, wearing different garish colors, carrying different rusty weapons. They demanded that we feed them. They were loud, and scornful of the loveliness of a young family. They took our baby from us at saber-point. They commented on how weirdly hot the child was, and repeated the order for a home-cooked meal. They couldn't stop laughing. They rested their boots on the table. They informed us that they came with the house . . . that they'd always be here, expecting us to feed them. Now why did we think such a nice house had been within our price range? Hadn't we ever stopped to wonder what might account for the bargain? Hadn't we noticed the shadow in the eye of the real estate agent?

Our baby began to shriek—we rushed toward our baby—they blocked us with their sabers—we shrieked too and—then our—baby—blew up like a—bomb glorious hot—fire smoke exploding and—we were left there with the—charred remains of nine pirates and—our beautiful empty house and—no physical evidence at all of the—child we'd once had—

the hauntings

haunting #1

Rumor has it that a magnificent trick takes place in our apartment, so the greatest magicians come to figure it out. Their hot-air balloons fill the sky, making our hearts do somersaults. They land on rooftops and dumpsters. They're an unkempt, smelly lot, with chaotic eyebrows. Sequins flake off their moth-eaten clothing. Their boots nick our wooden floors. They chew cloves of garlic. They squeeze in, all 112 of them, and the syllables of languages we've never heard pile up in our ears. Jammed together in our bathtub, we pinch our noses. An English-speaking magician finds us, yanks back the shower curtain, and says angrily, "Soooo?"

There is, in our apartment, a perfect glass globe that drifts around above our heads. When we're away, we think of it. When we return, we're happy to see it. Occasionally, however, it develops a crack. At first, this seemed to happen randomly, but eventually we realized what it correlates to . . . one crack becomes many cracks, and, in a brilliant crash of glass, the globe succumbs to gravity. Those nights are miserable. We lie stiffly beside each other, wondering how this happened to us, we who do not believe ourselves capable of feeling anything toward each other but love. We leave the shattered glass wherever it has fallen. We don't disturb a shard. Later, we wake to find the globe drifting merrily above us. Our limbs lose their stiffness. We put the teakettle on and begin to use words again.

Now, with 112 magicians surrounding us, we point to the globe hovering over the bathtub. "It cracks and mends, cracks and mends," we tell them, "but you'll have to wait for who knows how long." Impulsively, we dub the trick The Phoenix. "Bah!" they say. "Twenty-three tricks already have that name. And we don't see any globe, you big fools." They leave in a furious rush, filling the sky with hot-air balloons; and indeed the globe would never crack at a time like this (we're holding each other, we're laughing).

haunting #2

Every night we hear them—at least, we think we do. The sounds are just below the threshold of hearing, but sometimes they swell up. A sigh, a whispery movement. Fruitlessly, we strain to hear more. We wonder if these sounds seep into our sleep and account for our indecent dreams of red planets with purple skies, white seas filled with eager mermaids, black forests where aroused monsters roam. Indecent, yes, but can we deny that these frustrating, inaudible sounds make us smile in the dark? Ultimately, though, we conclude that they're infuriating. Still, we can't resist pushing our ears harder than we've ever pushed them, demanding so much of those tender organs that we can feel them trembling with the strain, deep inside our skulls—and suddenly we can hear everything. Something sliding moistly into something. Breaths. A nipple pinched between teeth. The desperate sigh that follows. Dirty, tender murmurs exchanged. It's intolerable to hear such things! It makes our hearts ache! We can hear the sweat slipping down their inner arms. *We can hear their goddamn skin cells rubbing off.* But then again—can we? Unsure, we put our ears to the wall. And now there's no doubt about it. Yes indeed, something's happening there on the other side. It must be stopped! We slide along the walls, trying to identify the exact location, but the sounds seem to be coming from everywhere. Well damn. We get our hammer. We remove our stupid, cheerful photographs and begin to demolish the wall. Plaster rains down upon us. We haven't had this much fun in—well, that's a sad thought.

Then—we break through the plaster. And what we discover. What we discover is. Our walls are not filled with insulation. No. They are filled with enormous guts. Intestines slowly oozing. Pink and wet. Enormous. They make beautiful, sensual noises as they move, slowly digesting whatever it is they're digesting. Clinging to each other, we fall back onto our bed, press our stomachs together, and (oddly, terrifyingly, finally) begin to desire each other again.

haunting #3

The beautiful old proverb lady tells us that when she moved into the large and elegant house of her third husband, his dead wife started to follow her around, looking over her shoulder while she whisked eggs, giggling softly if she slipped on the bathroom tiles, standing in the corner observing the nighttime antics in the bedchamber of the newlyweds. The husband, a doctor and a sensible man, left the proverb lady alone one evening, and then the dead wife really went to town! She ran her fingers creepily through the hair of the proverb lady; she bumped her arm so that a half-jar of ground ginger went into the delicate soup; she became water and gurgled furiously in the toilet bowl. The proverb lady ran through the house, turning on every light and flinging open every window. The husband returned to find his abandoned house throwing radiance and heat out into the dark cold night. Eventually, he seduced the beautiful old proverb lady back to him. At first she came hesitantly, like a chipmunk;

then forcefully, like a dragon. They installed themselves in a different large and elegant house, protected from ghosts by its curving walls (*EVIL SPIRITS ONLY WALK IN STRAIGHT LINES!*) and the network of ponds on its grounds (*EVIL SPIRITS CANNOT PASS OVER WATER!*). Confident in these superstitious measures, the beautiful old proverb lady became very happy and reasonable, and now can laugh about the night she fled the old house.

We, too, laugh. Firstly, because we adore the beautiful old proverb lady. Secondly, because we are exceedingly modern people and do not believe in ghosts or intangibles. We understand that love is transferable, and do not judge widowers for seeking joy somewhere. Yet unbeknownst to you, I laugh for a third reason: if you marry another woman after me, I will stand in the corner of the kitchen, staring at the two of you as you cook and eat. I will creep around the bedroom; I will run my fingers slowly through her terrible hair.

haunting #4

I am in love with an alien. This must be kept a secret. He's a slender, elegant alien in a gray suit. Alien love is different from human love. There's no infidelity in my loving the alien. He sits in the orange chair in our living room, legs crossed, gazing benevolently at me. Does he look human, you may wish to know. Well—yes and no. He has a head, a neck, two eyes, two arms, two legs, etc.; he wears a suit made for a man. Yet I wouldn't take him outside. He couldn't pass for one of us. His skin is grayer than ours, his limbs more elongated. But more importantly, he's not—how to put it?—not firm around the edges. The lines that define where he ends and where everything else begins—they're sort of blurry. So we're confined to the apartment, and the daytime, since at night he vanishes altogether. As the sun sets, his shape becomes ever less convincing, and by dark he is no more than a slight fragrance, which my husband scarcely notices upon returning home. "What's that smell?" he says. I say, "I used cloves in the stew."

You may wish to know how we met? I was sitting here, working, as always, and then there he was, in his elegant suit, in the chair. My heart choked. I guessed first that he was a murderer, then a rapist, a robber, a ghost; only on the fifth guess did I get it right. How do we spend our days? He watches me while I work, and while I cook. We listen to the radio, though music sometimes seems to jangle his ears. I nap, and he sits beside me, drinking water. He grins when I tell tender stories about my husband. And when I'm upset with my husband, he smiles sadly. He knows only six words of my language.

At midnight my husband says to me, "You're as beautiful as an alien." At noon the alien reminds me, "The beloved is always an alien."

haunting #5

In this home you'll find twenty-seven clocks nailed to the four walls. We thought it would be fine; when we received them, we accepted enthusiastically. But all the delicate tick-tocks are making us crazy, altering our heartbeats. Why do people give clocks as wedding gifts? Is time briefer once you're married? Does it need more dividing up until it turns into nothing?

Our home is a booth perched alongside an elevated section of train track. Strangers in passing trains might observe that this booth is caught inside a web of graffiti and has narrow, miserly windows. Perhaps they think, "What an awful home *that* would make." But it suits us just fine. *True coziness can be achieved only in juxtaposition with that which lacks all coziness.* We have one bed, two bowls, two cups. A bookshelf and a teakettle, a row of seashells and a quilt sewn by a witchy grandmother. We enjoy clinging to each other to stay warm.

Ok. To be honest. Sometimes it's not cozy. It's lonely and strange up here. As tidy as we keep our home, we're powerless against the blackish haze that creeps in through invisible cracks. Sometimes the electricity vanishes and the toilet fails to flush. Though we nuzzle deep into each other, still we wake stiff, cold, sad. And always those clocks nag at us.

Some nights we hear a mystifying voice. It says, *There's horses here for everyone.* This sentence fills us with a sensation we identify as nostalgia, though we've never in our life ridden a horse. *There's horses here for everyone.* We can think of no words more hopeful than these.

One frigid morning, we're awoken by an unfamiliar smell. We look out our window to the street far below. There, blocking traffic, is a herd of horses. Hundreds of them. They're enormous, forceful. We run down, down, until we're near them. Their rumps are strong and golden and chestnut and velveteen and powerful in the sunrise. Their hoofs make irregular tick-tock sounds on the pavement. They face west.

haunting #6

In this version of the story, I look at the clock in the night and it reads 3:21. I look at it a few minutes later. 3:16. A few minutes later, 3:53. Then, 2:47. I wake you. Something's wrong with our home. Odd things are always happening. Even time can't keep itself straight here. We conclude that it all must have the same source; in the predawn darkness we use miniature flashlights to search for irregularities, any cracks where hauntings might enter. (If only the man at table 14 were here to help!) Eventually we do discover an imperfection. Beneath the sun-stained couch, a gap between two floorboards; one gives a quiet creak and loosens. We yank at it, bloodying our fingernails. Then the gentlemanly floorboard springs upward, inviting us into the cavity beneath. We can't see what's down there, and it's not the kind of place into which one wishes to stick one's hand. "Let's make tea," I suggest, stalling. "And turn on some lights," you add. But neither of us stands. Instead, we reach into the darkness and feel something long, rectangular, plastic. We pull it out and recognize it: a sign, black, printed with white letters. CHAPEL. This belongs over the bureaucratic window in City Hall where marriage papers are signed. We replace the floorboard, drag the couch back, and return to bed.

Perhaps we've fixed the problem. Perhaps things will be different now.

But we have no confidence. Probably our assorted clocks will continue to behave strangely, dinging and donging at impossible moments, jumping around with no respect for time. Probably the CHAPEL sign will leave a rectangle of weird dust wherever we put it. We toss and turn. On the movie screen of my closed eyes I see fires sometimes, sometimes floods. Other times the screen is blank, or there's a whale or monster in the distance. You flop over in your sleep. I say to you the best thing I can think of. *The floodwaters are rising, yet we shall have a party.*

the monsters

monster #1

It is too terrifying to—
First I must describe the woods. They are soft and low; the trees are small; there are many ferns. These woods are the least dangerous woods. As children, my sister and I always had trouble working ourselves up into that pleasant state of fairytale fear—of a stepmother, a witch, a dragon—we wished to achieve. We stayed until nightfall, waiting for the trees to become malevolent, but they just stood there like grandmothers. Now, grown up, we've become grateful for the mildness of the woods. We go walking—discuss husbands and houses—but listen here! Listen here!:
Yesterday we saw a monster in the woods. We did. We did. Listen! This is not a story from a different era. This is not an attempt at metaphor or surrealism; this is not an attempt to drag mythology into the modern world. I am telling you: it is the year 2010, and yesterday, walking in the woods, my sister and I saw

a monster. He emerged from among the small trees. Our woods were as bright and undangerous as ever. The monster—he had skin the same color as ours, but it looked thick as an elephant's and hung heavily off his bones. His arms were long, his neck skinny. He would've been seven feet tall if he hadn't been stooped over, dragging his four-fingered hands along the ferns. He got so close that we could see his bloodshot eyes. He did not respond to us, but he was aware of us, like a commuter in a subway car. He was awful, I'm telling you. Patches of hair on his scalp. Between the legs there was nothing, smooth as a plastic doll.

It makes sense, doesn't it, that this is how they would appear, first penetrating our most gentle and unmagical places? I'll go out there today, and tomorrow, and the next day. I want to see him again and again, forever. I want to see his horrible self; this is what my sister and I were waiting for all along.

monster #2

The adults drink drinks and get nostalgic while in the other room the kids watch TV. They discover a channel showing a gray field stretching far into the distance beneath a gray sky. This might sound boring, but two things make it not boring. First, it's three-dimensional. It's so easy to believe this is not a TV screen but rather a window, and if you were to climb through, you'd be standing on that field. Second, way down the field, something is moving . . . coming forth. The kids stare at the screen, mesmerized. Elsewhere, the oblivious adults pour another round. They're getting so nostalgic! They're thinking of certain glowing green fields. Meanwhile, the thing keeps coming. As it gets closer, the youngest kids hide their whimpers beneath scornful declarations. "This is *boring*," they say. "Change the channel!" they chant. But the older ones enjoy the terror shooting through them. The thing's skin is gray and thick, hanging heavily off its bones.

Its arms are long, its neck skinny. It is very tall but it stoops, dragging its hands in the dirt. It has patchy hair on its scalp. It approaches them. When they see its bloodshot eyes, even the older kids want to change the channel. It looks at them too knowingly, as though it is aware of them, as though there's no TV screen between them and it. "Change the channel!" they command. Someone hits the button. The channel doesn't change. Someone hits it again. Still, no change. They pound the button. The thing is right there in the foreground. "You'll never be able to change it," it says in a high, weird voice. "Turn off the TV!" someone yells. Someone pushes the power button, but it won't turn off. "Unplug it!" someone yells. But even when the TV is unplugged, the thing remains. They scream. They feel its bloodshot eyes on them. When the nostalgic parents come to see what's going on, they find an empty room. On TV, a peaceful scene of a gray field.

monster #3

There is a creature in the park. It looks like an albino squirrel. It moves pure white and snakelike across branches. It seems to be a gentler sister to the dangerously white swans that drift, cruel and wonderful, across the brilliant black water of the lake. Once, looking upward in the usual spot on my daily walk, I saw it waiting there on a precarious branch above me, perfectly still. It gazed at me and I discovered that it had human eyes. I discovered that it knew me, and wished to know me better.

I have disliked animals—have used weapons against a blundering bat, have felt my gut turned to jelly by possums circling garbage—but this creature didn't evoke that prehistoric disgust.

Yesterday, as I searched the tapestry of leaves for a flash of white, the creature dashed out from the underbrush. Lifting one paw, it gazed coyly back at me, luring me into the woods. Honored, I followed my creature off the paved path, jumped a barbed wire fence. It led me into the untouched center of the park, into woods I couldn't have imagined—medieval woods, vines and mushrooms. The light grew darker, but my creature glowed. Eventually, it leapt into a bush, looked up at me, smiled—yes, smiled—and gestured downward with its neck. I noticed two things. First, my creature had wings! It spread them wide, bat-like but lace-like too, almost invisible. Second, there was a nest full of offspring that resembled small pieces of peeled pear, pale and slightly transparent. They squirmed over one another like slugs.

The creature darted its neck out and bit off the top of my index finger. It sprinkled my blood over its offspring. The red quickly faded to pink on their weird, pale skin. Then the creature swallowed my flesh. Shrieking, I examined my finger. No bone had been taken. I saw that it would heal. The creature cocked its head. And I became suddenly, desperately jealous of the creature that knows what needs to be done and does it.

monster #4

They live over the ridge, across two rivers, beyond the valley, past three meadows. They move fast. Their arms and legs are longer than ours. Their skin shines in the light of noon. They do not tire. At midday, we're forced into the shade. We lie there, small and hot and lazy, puffing out our empty bellies. They do not seem hungry. They notice us the way they notice the sun (which does not burn them) or the river (for whose water they do not thirst) or the stars (to whose mysteries they seem indifferent). Nothing could frighten them. This frightens us.

When we spot them, we ache for something for which we do not yet have a term; thousands of years from now, we will settle on the right word.

We cluster ourselves around the fire of a single consoling thought: We shall survive into the future, and they shall not. This fact has been passed back to us by a prophetess from the year 2010, and we know it is true. A second thought, less consoling because we do not know if it is true: We are more intelligent than they. We lie in the shade, thinking these things, convincing ourselves we are superior.

But say they pass near enough that we can make out their features. Say two of them, a male and a female, come striding radiant up the ridge. Their gaze drifts down over us, at once compassionate and severe. Silver eyes. Sharp noses. Bronze skin. The unconcerned calm of predators. Our men find themselves hardening. Our women go slick between the legs.

They each carry an object. These objects glow in the sun. What are they? Circles, someone says. Three-dimensional circles, someone adds. Globes, someone corrects. Spheres. Made of what? Rock. No, stone. No, marble. They made those? How did they make those? What are they for? No, quartz. No, obsidian. We could never make such a thing.

They vanish over the ridge, and we're left knowing foolish evolution will select us over them.

monster #5

A prehistoric girl walks into a convenience store in the year 2010, accompanied by a normal, modern young man. She has thick limbs and a large head, her features not yet entirely liberated from their origin in the face of a chimpanzee. She smells unfamiliar. No woman smells this way anymore. It's a smell that makes you want to figure out its source. She wears men's jeans, a t-shirt. Her feet are bare—which, unfortunately, could get her kicked out—but on second glance it appears she *is* wearing shoes, flip-flops lost beneath the wideness of her feet. Her hair is shiny like the fur of small mammals. She pushes it behind her ears with her big thumbs. Her skin is the color of almonds and resilient as plastic.

They go to the candy aisle. She paws the Butterfingers. He picks one up and places it in her palm. She studies it, squints at the royal blue, the golden yellow. It pleases her. But already he's prepared with Reese's Peanut Butter Cups!—Peppermint Patties!—Skittles!—M&Ms! She encounters each object as though she's found it after walking hundreds of miles in the forest. How aggressively brilliant it all is beneath the fluorescent lights. Starburst. Snickers. Nerds. Lifesavers. Tic-Tacs. A thousand colors never seen in nature.

The Neanderthal puts her hands up to protect her moist black marble eyes. She groans. He tries to embrace her, but she's vastly stronger than he, and when she shrugs him off he's thrown backward, off-balance. He leans against the wall of candy, breathing hard, wondering if this fantasy's gotten out of control. Moaning very softly, she strolls, or rather, *stalks* down the aisle. She strokes the rows of candy as one would stroke a newborn or diamonds, any impossible treasure. She wishes to touch the unimaginable colors. She will never allow herself to be separated from the astonishing beauty of the convenience store. When they come to remove her, she will cling shrieking to the wall of candy until it falls, its riches exploding across the floor.

monster #6

They live there in the middle of the traffic circle at the intersection of five major roads, on that small island of grass where the city long ago planted four crabapple trees in the name of beautification. Sometimes they can be seen scurrying dangerously across six lanes of traffic, arms outstretched, holding hands, the mother and the daughter (well, it's impossible to know for sure, but the smaller one is identical to the larger one, as though they're two versions of the same person) in their matching gray garments. Garment, that's the only word to describe what they're wearing—large shapeless things that nuns might have been forced to wear on a continent harsher than ours. In summertime, they rest quietly while the humid gasoline swirls around them. The grass is not well tended—how to get a lawnmower across six lanes of traffic?—so when they lie down in it, they vanish. Sometimes the mother sits upright with the daughter's head in her lap, but to the naïve viewer—and indeed isn't anyone whipping around a traffic circle a naïve viewer?—she could easily be mistaken for a piece of litter, a plastic bag snagged on branch. In the fall they harvest crabapples and feast. In wintertime, on desolate nights, it's possible to spot the tiny fire over which they roast rats seasoned with the dried chives that grow among the blades of grass. In springtime they cannot resist standing up and stretching. Glimpsed among the riotous blossoms of the crabapple trees, they are gaunt. Their faces pale and simple, like snow.

Many facts remain unknown. How they dispose of their bodily wastes. What happens when they run out of rats, crabapples, chives. What happens when it snows. Where they get water. When they last bathed. Why they never look unclean. Their names. Their birthplaces. If they speak English. If they are human. If they are happier than we are. If they know we've spent our whole lives wondering what it would be like to live in the middle of the traffic circle.

monster #7

I see her everywhere, the Old World lady who wears girlish pink lipstick, nightmarish high heels, and a silk scarf around her neck like the woman in the fairytale whose head was held on only by a silk scarf. Her hair, bleached blonde for decades, looks like a nest for some species of small mammal we don't have on this continent. When she scratches her head, the sound of her fingernail moving across her scalp is audible.

I see her in airport security, where they screen her because she's incapable of looking innocent. Her head thrown back atop her stiff neck, she permits them to pat her down. I see her in the subway, wrapped in a fur coat that appears faux or genuine depending on the light. I see her in the courtroom, translating the defendant's words from Russian into English, proudly wrapping her tongue around both languages. She rarely blinks. I see her in the grocery store, buying sixteen grapefruits. Is it the same Old World lady every time, or are there many of them? The snarl of hair remains constant, the extravagant shoes, the avoidance of eye contact.

I have always been frightened of monsters, have spotted them stalking through the woods and crouching under the bed. Gargoyles on old buildings howl at me. I'm susceptible. Monsters wish to haunt me; I see her everywhere.

I've been instructed to confront my fears by following her home. Surely her apartment is the apartment of an alcoholic, dusty and incomplete, where even the brightest colors become dull. When I slip in the door behind her, she'll take off her neck scarf and her head will tumble to the floor. Then again. Maybe her apartment is the apartment of a grandmother. A kitchen with yellow walls. She removes her shoes and dons slippers. Beneath her wig there's a demure little bun. She brews tea. She tells me about the monsters she had to fight in the Old World, and explains the various methods a woman can use to overcome them.

monster #8

He and She lived in a precise garden composed of four equal quadrants and an octagonal fountain. Numerical precision is one way to honor God. There was a crabapple tree in each quadrant, and in each a different set of herbs: Culinary, Magic, Love, Poisonous. These herbs served their purposes effortlessly: pluck a sprig of mint, and a cup of mint tea would appear in your hand. Wave a stalk of goldenrod at a threatening sky, and the storm would disperse. Bring an iris to your beloved during a disagreement, and both of you would start laughing. They didn't know what the poisonous herbs were for; when those herbs were picked, nothing happened.

The garden was surrounded by a cloistered walkway. After many years of examining the carvings on the stone pillars, it became possible to decipher narratives, some wonderful and some inexplicable. It was pleasant to sit on the stone benches protected by the cloister. And beyond the cloister? A high and impenetrable stone wall.

One afternoon, She fell into the dark dreamless sleep of the first woman; there were no landscapes yet to illuminate her dreams, no creatures to inhabit them. When She woke, He was gone. He was nowhere, absolutely nowhere. He'd never been out of her sight. She felt it in her chest, on the mysterious left side. She grabbed herbs and thrust them at the blackening sky, but nothing. Nothing.

Suddenly She recalled the pillar they'd never been able to make sense of. This pillar had carved into it their unmistakable garden itself. But the garden was empty; the crabapple trees bare; the herbs shriveled; and, in the shadow of the cloister, *indeed hiding behind the very pillar into which this scene was carved*: a monster made of faces. His face was a face, his torso was a face, each arm was a face, his hands and feet were faces, his legs were faces. For the first time ever, She screamed, and in the garden the leaves of the crabapple trees began to turn gray.

the regimes

regime #1

They come in the night. I, who sleep naked, stand up wrapped in a sheet.

"Ten minutes," they say. They throw a suitcase on the floor. "You can bring whatever fits in here. We'll wait outside."

The quilt my aunt made, which could keep me warm wherever we're going? But that would fill the suitcase entirely. Socks and underwear, a toothbrush? But what a waste of space on necessities. The green party dress my mother bought me, the most expensive item I own, and attached to certain memories of certain nights? But how frivolous. The thirty-three notebooks I once filled with poetry, which in another era were my most precious possession?

Outside, they stomp their boots. "Eight minutes, sweetheart!" they shout.

The time has come to be sensible. I put on four pairs of underwear, two pairs of socks, jeans, sneakers, three t-shirts, a long-sleeved shirt, a sweatshirt, a coat. Hat, scarf, gloves. But I've done it all wrong!

I should layer my joyous skirts under my green party dress. I should tape notebooks of poetry to my stomach. And the suitcase is still empty.

"Three minutes, baby!"

Too late now! It's got to be my books. It doesn't take long to fill the suitcase with Neruda and Shakespeare. But when I try to lift it, it falls lopsided out of my grasp. The books splay across the floor. Then I remember my essential medications. They're in the secret dresser drawer, beside my wooden jewelry box, which reminds me of the pearl necklace my mother left me when she died!

They come up the stairs. "Ready or not," they say. They open the door. "Apparently not," they say when they see the disarray of the room. I cling to the dresser, hot, bundled, my medications rolling on the floor at my feet, the strand of pearls dangling from my hand.

"Ok," they say, grabbing me. "No suitcase for you. Let's hit the road."

Tomorrow night, they will come again. And the next night. And the next. And the next.

regime #2

There was a photographer who lived in a city with many spires. The problems he faced were small and delightful. At what angle should the bride tip her parasol? How to get thirty schoolchildren silent and smiling for one second? Where to direct an old woman's chin so as to remind the viewer of her as a girl? How to capture a lull in the screams of an infant, transform the simper on the face of a teenager, prevent a toddler from tearing down the velvet drapes. He had many painted backgrounds (a meadow in the Alps, a street in Paris, an Italian villa, a barnyard, the principal cathedral in this selfsame city) and chests of props: scarves, teddy bears, plastic ferns.

Times changed. The photographer was instructed to remove the colorful backgrounds from his walls. People were brought to him in the night. They ran up to him, pulled on his sleeves, asked questions. His was the first unmasked face they had seen since all this began. But he knew nothing, said nothing. Their clothing was to be removed. They were to be photographed in three different positions. How sadly their genitals and breasts hung. He did certain things. Emphasized warm sepia hues when developing the film. Allowed the littlest children to hold a teddy bear while they were photographed. Allowed the shyest women to keep their undergarments on. He was punished severely for doing these things, and then no longer did them.

One night, a very weak woman was brought in. The photographer recognized her. They'd gone to grade school together. Her hair had smelled like graham crackers. She had been skilled at drawing perfect circles. Now her hair was falling out in patches. Her breasts were extraordinarily small and her hips extraordinarily wide.

The next night, a very weak woman was brought in. The photographer recognized her. They'd gone to grade school together.

The next night, a very weak woman was brought in. The photographer recognized her.

The next night, a very weak woman was brought in.

regime #3

In our city, there was a museum. In that museum, there was a section of wall from an ancient house. A fresco, the sign informed us, from an inner courtyard. We'd stare at that fresco for many long minutes. "*How* can you be so red, 2,058 years later?" we wanted to ask it, and did, speaking very softly so as not to seem eccentric. Three elements were depicted in the fresco: a pale yellow courtyard floor, five pale green columns, and that red, red wall behind. It made our heads spin, the realization that this fresco rendering a courtyard was once part of a courtyard. But wait—in fact there were four elements depicted—in the fresco's bottom left corner, we spotted the delicate outline of a grape-leaf. This grape-leaf disrupted the perfect symmetry, and we became immediately fond of it. Suddenly we understood that the creator of this fresco had been mischievous, like us, and we wished we could have bought him a beer. We'd have asked him "*How* can you be so red, 2,058 years later?", drunkenly confusing the artist with the product, and he'd have answered our question as though he were the fresco itself, saying with a grin, "I am so red 2,058 years later because—"

There was something else in that museum that got to us. It was the marble centerpiece of an ancient fountain. It consisted of a man's face, eyes wide open, mouth stretched in the largest, most desperate scream ever. Looking at it, one could almost hear the scream. It was not a pleasant object, and though we could not resist its pull, we turned away as quickly as possible. *So gratuitous*, we thought to ourselves, wishing to return to the courtyard within the courtyard.

But when the soldiers invade the museum, the expression on the fountain's face ceases to be gratuitous. The fountain screams as the fresco comes crashing down, as the soldiers make off with brilliant red fragments. Across the city, trapped in dim, stifling rooms, we suddenly become capable of evil.

regime #4

During a terrible war, a woman sits alone in an auditorium. On the stage are two men. Both men look exactly like her husband. One is her husband. The other is an imposter, a talented actor whose skills have been co-opted by the regime for this very game. She must identify one of them as her husband. If she picks correctly, her husband will hop off the stage, will stroll with her to their apartment, will eat the illegal pear she's been saving for the occasion. Their home will smell richly of black-market coffee; they'll sit on the sun-stained couch while the sun sinks. If she picks incorrectly, her husband will be shot in the plaza.

The men wear identical black sweaters, jeans, sneakers. Both are six days' unshaven. Both are equally tall. Both have dark hair, brown eyes. Both have a wrinkle running vertical between their eyebrows. Both have clammy skin under the stage lights. At first they stand before her with bowed heads, as though each expects her to recognize him immediately. There's no hint coming from one that does not also come from the other. The slight sloping of the shoulders, the slight curve in the spine: these markers that lie in the skeleton itself do not help her, for one of these men has studied the other and understands everything about his body. They may say only one word. It must be the same word, agreed upon beforehand, spoken simultaneously. They say it, and she stiffens; she has not been called this in a while. But it doesn't serve as a clue. They both look at her with imploring, tender eyes. Shouldn't she be able to see on his face, like a filmstrip playing across it, the memories to which only he and she are privy?

She is given one minute in which to make her decision. The loudspeakers inform her that fifteen seconds remain. Both men gaze at her with familiar, infinite, identical love. Slowly, terribly, she raises her arm, unfurls her finger, and points.

regime #5

Please be warned that an essential piece of information will be withheld from you until the very last instant. In the meantime, your heart will beat too quickly. You'll wake parched and unsure.

In order to distract yourself from this circumstance, we strongly recommend that you pile everything you own in the living room. When your spouse reacts with dismay, pretend you're not daunted by what you've done. Maintain a cheerful, flippant exterior. Adhere to the following guidelines: Get rid of an object if it's been over a year since you used it, if it has holes, if it's a meaningless wedding gift, a knickknack, a birthday card, a magazine, a CD, a book . . . Don't you feel better already? Now's the time to disregard your spouse's scared, compassionate eyes, to playfully salute your spouse, shouting "Hiya there, sport, howdya like the mighty wind of change blowin' through our digs?" Continue to work even as your spouse stares at you. Don't be surprised if your spouse goes to the kitchen, maybe even to the liquor cabinet, and doesn't return for a long time, if ever. You'll come upon things that initially strike you as magical (Christmas lights encased in scallop shells, red bracelets from faraway continents, a plastic eggplant), but don't be seduced by such ephemera. Gather these "precious" objects and take them to the street. Let the vultures descend in the form of your neighbors. When everything's gone except a few old shirts, don't let those shirts—slumping over the sides of the cardboard boxes, their arms splayed in gestures of supplication—pull on your heartstrings. Somebody will claim them soon; no guarantees about who it will be, nor how that person will treat them, but this is precisely what we are trying to teach: Avoid sentimentality. Don't get bogged down in your emotions; remember, they're just chemicals and synapses.

It is at this time that the crucial piece of information will no longer be withheld. Now we'll reveal to you the exact instant at which you shall ___.

regime #6

Because our government is concerned about the low number of infants being produced by our population on an annual basis, a National Reproduction Day is declared, and the lights in the subways are turned to their lowest, rosiest setting. Slender white candles are given out free of charge. All married citizens of childbearing age are ordered to stay home. It is mandated that liquor stores remain open until midnight the evening before. Chocolate and strawberries are sold half price. The streets are strewn with rose petals. The aged and unmarried members of the Symphony play Tchaikovsky's most extravagant melodies in the square. Young wives are informed that the Prime Minister wishes them to wear their most provocative garments to the breakfast table. Young husbands are reminded that women are most sensitive at the nape of the neck. Banners containing romantic slogans are hung across the highways.

But I don't wear anything provocative to the breakfast table. Instead, in honor of National Reproduction

Day, we sit naked on our sun-bleached couch. Your penis is limp and my breasts sag, as though we are already old. We hear strains of Tchaikovsky stretching down the alleyways; we notice the sadness beneath the lushness. The sun casts pale, unvigorous light across the wooden floor. We conclude, somewhat smugly, that we are different from everyone else. We do not wish to drink champagne at this hour. We are not particularly grateful to have a day blocked off for this purpose. It happens to us bizarrely, while washing the dishes or upon waking from nightmares. Honestly, we'd rather do laundry today. But if we were to be seen outside—a young, healthy, fertile couple—surely we would be apprehended and sent back to our bedroom. Even so! We gather our laundry; heavily laden, rebellious, nervous, snapping at each other and then apologizing, we make our way through the empty, moaning city until we find an open laundromat. It is packed with many young, healthy, fertile couples, heavily laden, rebellious, nervous, snapping at each other and then apologizing.

regime #7

They order us to grow raspberries on our windowsills. We don't know what motivates this law. We do know it's been a long time since supermarkets carried raspberries; our children wouldn't recognize them. Our memories flit around something: a hill somewhere, raspberry brambles over fragrant dirt, a thrilled, frightened person, the unfamiliar sensation of abundance, a stomachache, a good night's sleep. This is the extent of our knowledge about raspberries—so how can we be expected to grow them ourselves? We lose sleep over this, as over everything. Restless and sad, we search the cupboards of cramped kitchens where no moonlight reaches.

Raspberry seeds arrive in government envelopes. We're embarrassed by our overwhelming feeling of gratitude. We praise the regime for being so organized. Another blessing: the seeds come with instructions. We obey. We buy pots and dirt, sweating in long supermarket lines. If the stakes were lower, we'd let our children plant the seeds but, under the circumstances, we do it with our own trembling fingers.

There's a certain pleasure in watering the dirt while our children look on with thrilled, frightened eyes. Yet as the weeks pass, we curse the weak sunlight, so unlike the thick sunbeams of our childhood. Alone, at night, we pray they put families in one prison cell. And then: most joyous day. A green shoot. The following months are the best in recent memory. Things grow and unfurl. Our children clap and hoot. We try to enjoy their happiness without reflecting on the fact that they're too easily impressed. Suddenly, miraculously: three tiny hard green raspberries. Breathless, we watch the slow blush spread. Soon men with guns will appear, asking for raspberries, and we—we shall deliver! We teach our children to do somersaults across the bed. The raspberries become large and bright, sagging on green stems, desirable.

So when the knock comes at our door, when we rush to fetch our three raspberries, it's hard to know who to blame, who to hate, since we've all considered eating them at one time or another.

regime #8

When the man in the navy blue suit returned to the town, this is what he found: a tangle of dead rose-bushes, blossoms shriveled like the ears of old women, a metallic sound as hot wind moved among the thorns. He stood there in fury. His briefcase slipped from his perspiring fingers. He fell asleep and dreamed of an air-conditioner. A white hotel room. A place where a plan was hatched to save a nation. After a few seconds, he awoke and collected himself. He picked up his briefcase. He knocked on every door. No one answered. Curtains flickered in upstairs rooms. This town—it was a coy woman vanishing into a dying rose bramble.

"Townspeople!" he shouted. "Dear townspeople!" He fell asleep and dreamed of someone slipping off the back of a stampeding giraffe. A funny, horrible dream. He awoke. "I would have changed your lives!" he cried out.

He still had his charts and his graphs, and was tempted to pull them out again. He'd shown them here months ago, right in this very place, to a crowd of skinny, nervously laughing townspeople. He'd spoken of the benefits of perfume versus opium; he'd evoked for them regal women ravenous for expensive rose-based fragrances with which to cover their animal odors. Sweating, he'd brought forth infant rosebushes from the van in which he'd journeyed hundreds of miles over sandy roads. But his beautiful charts and graphs—they'd already been used here—they were no longer potent—now they were merely paper and colored ink—humbly explaining and expounding upon the best idea anyone had ever had.

Yet look at this. These roses. Crippled, curled like fetuses.

The man in the navy blue suit dropped his briefcase. He fell asleep and dreamed of a field of such red poppies. They were enormous, exploding. They had no fragrance, yet the color itself resembled a smell. It was tempting, then irresistible, to step forth. He awoke. There was a field of red poppies. Among them stood one skinny townsperson, staring at him with angry, puzzling eyes.

regime #9

Rumors fly. "The average citizen, during sleep, eats eight spiders over the course of a lifetime" . . . "eats ten spiders each month" . . . "eats twenty-five spiders each night." We're uncomfortable, afraid; we wonder what these spiders want with us. Desiring truth and order, an anonymous benefactor hires a fleet of detectives. These detectives can pick any lock. They wear black garments that make them invisible after dark. They are respectful and professional. Respectfully, they break into homes across the nation; make their way down hallways; enter bedrooms. Sometimes they take the liberty of gently pulling on the chin of a closed mouth, opening it to the ideal position. After pushing away stuffed animals and strewn clothing, they crouch beside beds. They watch. They wait. They gather statistics. Before leaving, they return our objects to the original messy position. The detectives sigh at the chaos of our bedrooms; it's not pleasant for them to see how we live, for they are meticulous men, tidy, precise, as evidenced by the dense numbers on their graph paper.

Sometimes, though, there's a detective who, unbeknownst to himself, has two minutes' worth of dreaminess in him. A random bedroom, a random citizen, mouth flung open, moonlight glowing on teeth. Shimmering with saliva, a pathway into the velvet darkness of the interior. The tongue as welcome mat. One senses the interior calling to oneself. One imagines oneself traveling up the neck, around the chin, over the lip. In short, one begins to think like a spider. Horrified, the detective rises from his crouch, knocking over a lamp. Ought he add another mark to the graph paper, or ought he not? Did a spider enter this mouth, or did it not? He doesn't know! *He has never not known!* In the morning, someone is bemused to find the lamp fallen, the bathrobe folded, a sheet of graph paper covered in meaningless markings.

The results of this study are never made public. They are inconclusive, revealing nothing, and many good men were ruined in the process.

regime #10

In our country, where many things have been decreed, it has now also been decreed that laundry may not be hung outside to dry. No straight answer will be given us as to why, but surely it has something to do with eyesores and property values, dryer manufacturers and electricity corporations. Meanwhile, our clotheslines sway longingly in the breeze, gleam mournfully in the sunlight. We crave the stiffness of clothing dried outside. We've always believed there's nothing quite as wistful as a clothesline hung with the garments of an entire family—bright colors and dull, striped, checkered, paisley, polka-dotted, flapping over the backyards, telling stories through large bras and small pajamas and holey undershirts. Not to mention clothespins! They look so archaic, and serve their purpose so single-mindedly. They remind us of long, weird insects, or of can-can girls with more leg than torso. At the laundromat, we sigh as we drop coins in the dryer. Those damn dryers! They devour quarter after quarter and then our laundry emerges fuzzy and shrunken.

Today, an old woman in our neighborhood hung her laundry out to dry. Her huge wonderful underwear looks like the handkerchiefs of gods, up there against the blue sky. We see her lavender sheets, her black dresses, her unrecognizable undergarments from another century (the word 'bustier' comes to mind, and 'girdle,' though we're unclear on all of it). We stand in our backyards, staring. How satisfying to see, after this awful hiatus, a clothesline in use. We watch her clothing dry like those folks who watched paint dry. The wind tugs on her odd undergarments. Her lavender sheets swell like the bellies of pregnant women. Her black dresses roast and steam in the sun. We use her clothing for clues: it proves that she has lost her husband, that she is very lonely, that she is indestructible. By the time her laundry is nearly dry, she is dear to us, but already the furious sirens are howling several blocks away, and soon she will no longer be among us.

regime #11

Tourists from our country are astonished to discover that here, in your country, light does not have density. Our grandparents spoke longingly of a time when the light in our country did not weigh down on everyone. This is why we go to your greatest bridge. We walk to the middle, where those stone archways reach upward. We put down our snakeskin suitcases, still papered with stamps from customs. We take off our brown felt hats and finger the rims. We observe the way the sun strikes the cables of the bridge. These cables seem far too delicate, gleaming in sunbeams, to do what they're doing. We look at the water, where the light becomes playful, glinting in and among tiny waves. For us, it is all so difficult to believe. A wind swells up and blows litter in our direction: a discarded ice-cream sandwich wrapper, a yellow plastic bag, a fistful of lettuce covered in mustard. These objects glisten in the light, and we are delighted. "Icey creamy sandiewichie," we say in our embarrassing accents.

Then we turn our attention to the people of your country. We notice that the beautiful young boys and beautiful young girls wear large sunglasses to hide their eyes from the beautiful light. Imagine that! These girls and boys walk in slow motion, letting the wind do what it wishes with their skirts and t-shirts. We do not understand why your young people are not smiling. And we get worried when we see the young boys pressing the young girls against the glowing cables of the bridge. We picture the worst: lean beautiful bodies shooting toward the water, illuminated for a few seconds by the incredible sun. We have the urge to chide the boys: "Boy be you careful Girl!"

But then we remember that we are in a country where such things do not happen, where light is not heavy, where sun and wind and water and cables interact without agony, where the young cannot simply fall off great bridges into bright water.

the punishments

punishment #1

In the subway, you're somewhere on the spectrum from fat to skinny, old to young, ugly to beautiful. Like thousands of others, you have dark hair, decent posture, a zit, a cold, a chip on your shoulder. Like thousands of others, you have light hair, bad posture, bloodshot eyes, a hangover, a pleasant disposition, a fetus growing inside you. Like thousands of others, you're stuffed, you're hungry, you've hurt someone terribly, someone has hurt you terribly. You and a hundred men are trying to read the newspaper. You and a hundred women are trying to decipher the graffiti. It is peaceful. You are not the radiant resplendent unique individual they lied about when you were in preschool. Children shriek with delight or rage as they swing around the poles in the subway car, and it's obvious that all children are the same child. You lean back in the plastic seat. Tired, like everyone.

Then he boards the train. He wears purple sweatpants, beat-up sneakers, a tuxedo jacket, a bowtie. His face is two-weeks unshaven. His haircut is elegant. There's something evil in his face; you're grateful for the anonymity of the subway. He's the kind of man who carries the invisible knives of a criminal, or the invisible badge of a government spy. If he's not dangerous in one way, he's dangerous in the other. You sit in your seat like any person sitting in a seat.

But. He comes toward you. The other passengers shrink away, letting your uniqueness shine. He smells like a gorilla wearing cologne. It is you, exactly you, that he's here for. His teeth are yellowed just for you, to that same sunny color as the walls of your childhood kitchen. He has long eyelashes and long nosehairs. He stands above you. Your heart is a fawn, tripping over the underbrush as it tries to escape. It stumbles, falls. You have been found. Your heart beats in your brain like a hand pounding hard on a door in the middle of the night.

punishment #2

They came to my door, badges gleaming, and spoke scornfully. "Good afternoon, miss. We have some questions for you." These men already hated me, and I wondered what it was they thought I'd done. I was willing to believe them over myself; they were so tall, their hair so sleek. "What happened as you rounded that curve in the dirt road?" I did recall something miniscule: I'd driven over a branch—yes, I'd sensed it under the wheels. I told them this, and their eyes got cruel. "You hit and killed a woman and her little girl." At that instant, I exited myself and stayed away for many years.

When I return to myself, I'm trudging down a familiar dirt road alongside a familiar snowy field. It's far below zero. There should be a red barn in the field. My whole life it has always been there; the single most cheerful sight in the universe. But the barn is gone. They could have devised no crueler punishment. It's dangerous to cry in this weather. One's eyelids begin to freeze shut.

"Don't cry," someone says—the voice of a mother. Then I notice them beside me in the falling snow. I recognize them immediately, though I've never before seen them. They both look so peaceful, passing barefoot among the snowflakes in their summer dresses. I wish I, too, could stroll through the blizzard in a summer dress. I feel disinclined to apologize. They're better off than I. "It's just that there's a man involved," the woman says mournfully. "Otherwise, it wouldn't matter. He burns his toast every morning." "You think I have a responsibility to your husband?" I say meanly. Awful things must have happened to me over the years; I've become unkind.

There was a man involved on my end as well. He was touching my face as I rounded that curve. He was saying something that seemed essential.

I turn back to discuss this matter further, but they've vanished. On the telephone wire, four inches of snow; three blackbirds taking flight.

punishment #3

I'm the kind of irksome girl who replies "I am feeling fabulous today, thank you" when asked "What's up?"; who devours virtuous, fibrous foods as though she enjoys them; who lists her blessings on fingers and toes; whose stupidly wiggling limbs fail to embarrass her when she dances.

Eventually, the villagers can't stand me any longer. They cast me out. And they're in the right. How right they are is proven by the good-natured way I take to the road, three teabags and two bran muffins in my knapsack. Against their better judgment, some of the mothers ask if I shouldn't include something more in the way of creature comforts. "Creature comforts!" I yelp merrily. Reassured yet again of my irritating eccentricity, my incapacity to feel shame, they turn their backs. Little do they know that a half-hour down the road I'm whispering to myself "comforts creature comforts creature comforts" and weeping because there is nothing in my life that resembles a creature (small, sleepy, furry, warm), nothing in my life that resembles a comfort.

I develop regrets: I should've acted disgruntled, disguised my enthusiasm, bitten my tongue, worn a poker face. These regrets fly above my head like crows. They wait darkly on telephone wires. Sometimes I think to myself, "Maybe those aren't regrets. Maybe there really are crows." Then I think, "That's the kind of thinking that gets you in trouble." I go from village to village, settling briefly in each before they realize that I'm the kind of irksome girl who X, Y, Z. Understandably, they cast me out.

One day, I see a boy in the marketplace. He has a large, stupid head and buckteeth. He presses his nose aggressively into a bundle of those cheap white flowers that have no scent. "They smell pretty," he says to nobody. Then, noticing me staring, he addresses me: "They smell pretty." Thereafter, he and I try to restrain ourselves from parading our glee in front of everyone, but sometimes it's impossible to rein in our high, stampeding laughter.

punishment #4

Because of everything that's happened, they're forced to settle in a small square suburban house. Adam, driven by natural instinct, tends the lawn. He even figures out the lawnmower. Eve, however, almost burns the house down when she attempts to use the stove. She declares she won't eat anything until she can eat fruit right off trees in their own yard. There are no trees at all in their yard, much less any fruit trees. Quickly, they learn the difference between making love and fucking. Afterward, Eve cries. She walks through the rooms, recalling the clean golden light of the other place. Here, the air is velvety with car exhaust.

Much to their surprise, Eve has a baby. They didn't know anything about anything. They'd assumed she was getting fat from all the potato chips he bought at the gas station since she refused to cook. But then one day she starts to feel large, dangerous things happening in her gut. Adam is still a slow and nervous driver; by the time they get to the hospital, the upholstery is soaked with Eve's blood.

They do the things they're supposed to do. They send their sons to school. Eve learns how to cook, and how to operate the dishwasher. She buys makeup. Adam works as a landscaper. He wears a baseball cap. They have their neighbors over for barbeques. They take photographs of their sons on prom night. Eve develops heavy jowls and sharply plucked eyebrows. She dyes her hair dark brown, almost black. She learns how to laugh heartily, and prefers jellied fruit to raw fruit.

One evening, the sunset in the suburbs is uncharacteristically golden.

"Hey," Adam says when Eve hands him a beer, "does this remind you of anything?"

"Honey," she says, "that goddamn dryer isn't—"

"Doesn't this remind you of anything?"

"Sure, baby," she says, "it reminds me of a nice sunset." There's nothing else it could remind her of, because she was born and raised in the suburbs, and this is all she's ever known.

the droughts

drought #1

Our parents say Get ready, it's time to go to the ruin. The what? The ruin. The ruin? The womb of civilization. The *what*?

Getting ready consists of rubbing our bodies with red mud. This mud dries on our skin and we look like aliens. Our parents lead us through a cactus graveyard. Cactus skeletons are sharp and black. We long for a living cactus. The sun dislikes the fact that we have protected our skin with dirt. It attempts to penetrate us, and sometimes it succeeds. The trail goes straight up among stunted and indifferent junipers. We are weary. Our parents are not. We try to take refuge in the smoky smell of sagebrush. We are thirsty. Water is not permitted. The earth is yellow, dry, red, dry, orange, dry, and dry. We wonder if the ancient peoples were more beloved than we. Our parents abandon the trail. Following them, we step over the bones of prairie dogs and swallows.

Our parents stop, and sigh. They have joyous expressions on their faces. We look around. Everything is the same. Dirt and sage. What is it? we say. What is it? we demand. The ruin, they say. Where? we say. Right there, they say. I don't see anything, we say. Oh, they say, did we forget to mention that the ruin is imaginary? Imaginary! we say. They say: Don't you love the tidy little houses? Don't the girls look beautiful fetching water in their dresses made of feathers? Aren't the young men beautiful too? Mom, we say. Dad. This is such a goddamn disappointment.

We pull out our forbidden water bottles. We drink, and wash ourselves until the dirt turns back to mud. We put on American sunblock and sunglasses. We tell our parents we're leaving. They do not respond. They do not follow us.

Someday we will bring our children here. We will say Get ready, it's time to go to the ruin. They will say The what? The *what*? We will come again; we will not be disappointed.

drought #2

"Isn't it *beautiful*?" they say proudly, gazing out over the landscape. Politely, I nod, though it looks like a wasteland to me. I want to ask them, "How long has it been since it even rained here?" They say, "The horizon seems *so far* away. Isn't that amazing!" Their enthusiasm is touching, childish. Imitating them, I put my hand to my heart in a gesture of awe. Unfortunately, though, I'm not awed by all these empty fields. I stare instead at a single black tree cowering under the enormous sky. I'd like to sit beneath that tree and make it feel useful once again so it would produce extravagant leaves. "*Gosh*!" they say cheerily, to fill the silence. "Gosh!" I reply. The empty granaries are lined up tidily like the toys of a foolish, anxious child. I don't tell them that these dry streambeds show up in my dreams; I fly unsteadily above white dust where water ought to run, imagining a trickle of dirty water, followed by a torrent, followed by fishes, brown speckled gold, green algae flowing like a girl's hair, a boat made from a leaf, someone dozing, someone whispering *Come here!*

But moreover I see the ragtag armies of the future marching dangerously across these plains, chanting cruel songs in languages that bear no relation to the languages of this era. They're always thirsty. They wear garments made from the pelts of animals that do not yet exist. They smear black blood on their skin to protect it from the evil sun. Their women lay eggs rather than gestating, and their offspring emerge slimy, weary, already starving. It's enough to make one shiver.

Misunderstanding me, as usual, they smile when they note the shiver passing through me. Surely I am reacting to the sunbeams that have just cut through the clouds, glorious sunbeams now stretching across the plains, illuminating the fields. "Don't those sunbeams look like they're made out of *matter* rather than light?" they say. "Maybe there really *is* something divine watching over this planet."

drought #3

This must be the time of year when baby birds fail, for I have seen them plastered to the sidewalk. From a distance they look like brown crumpled leaves, and you wonder how autumn snuck into spring, but then, when you're right on top of them, you see the agony of bent legs and soft bones and black fuzz and incomplete wings stuck to pavement. What oblivious passersby have stepped on the dead birds, pressing them flat? Have you ever done it, or have I?

The doctor says women who feel a lack when they don't menstruate are irrational. That's exactly what we're trying to do here, she says, make ourselves infertile for the time being. Right? She tells me that once, and only once, she knew a girl who lost her period and never got it back. I wonder if I am that girl. I never minded being reminded that there was a red world inside. And yet.

Springtime was born to strive; it strives against the

exhaust of trucks, against gynecologists in air-conditioned rooms, against broken lawn chairs stranded in the city park. The sun rises red and violent across the still water of the lake where seven swans glide eerily. I have come upon yellow swamp irises growing in the park. I know a place where an enormous tree fell in lightning, its solar system of leaves crashing down.

When I was a little girl they told me half of my daughter already existed, in a sac inside of me, for girls are born with all the eggs they'll ever have. I was told my daughter would wait there until the proper moment, and then would emerge. New science suggests this model is not accurate. Yet I think of my daughter, fidgeting, impatient, pimpled yet pretty, already a teenager but still inside of me, waiting, waiting. If only this planet could be trusted. If only these deserts would stop spreading. If only my daughter were here among us already, because I am no longer certain of anything.

drought #4

Buy This Sea SALT! Born From The Warm Waters Of The Mediterranean Sea, Each Crystal Contains The Energy Of The Sun. Our SALT Is Collected By Hand, Then Prepared In An Ancient And Secret Phoenician Tradition. This SALT Will Help You. A Man And Woman Sit At A Table, Nothing Between Them But A Small Bowl Of SALT. They've Just Eaten An Avocado With SALT, Or A Tomato With SALT. They Smile. He Reaches For Her And Knocks Over The SALT. They Each Take A Pinch And (Admiring The Large Crystals) Throw It Over Their Shoulders. No Bad Luck Descends On Them Ever! But You're Still Wondering About The Aforementioned Secret Phoenician Tradition! What A Curious Little Monkey You Are, Dear SALT-Buyer! You're Picturing A Black-Haired Woman In A White Dress, Stomping Around In An Enormous Wooden Vat of SALT. You Are So Imaginative! But That Is, Obviously, An Image Stolen From The Little You Know About The Making Of Wine. The Making Of SALT

Does Not Involve The Legs Of Mediterranean Women. However, Rest Assured That Our Phoenician Tradition Is Even More Charming. Enough Said. Shake This Box Until The SALT Sounds Like Rain. (Yes, Standing Right There In The Aisle Of The Supermarket. You Really Must Do Things Like This More Often. Have A Bit Of Fun In Life.) In This Drought-Ridden Time, Humans Need To Hear The Sound Of Rain. Now You Can Keep That Sound In Your Very Own Kitchen! You're Dancing, Aren't You, To The Rhythm Of The SALT? You Still Have A Certain Youthful Enthusiasm. It's Beautiful To Sea. Oops. "See," Not "Sea." But "Sea" Brings Us Back To Sea SALT. This SALT Will Save You. Sample One Crystal, Though If The Supermarket Gives You Trouble Don't Blame Us. Isn't It Satisfying, The Gem-Like Shape Of The Crystal In The Palm Of The Hand? And The SALTiness As You Crush It Between Your Molars. You Don't Need To Say It. We Know You Feel Better Now Than You've Been Feeling. Buy This Sea SALT!

drought #5

At the baths, naked women attempt to wash away their unhappiness in six stages: dry sauna, wet sauna, hot pool, cold pool, high shower, low shower. "Cucumber salves inner wounds." Always thirsty, they drink cucumber water in huge, vulgar gulps, and still they are thirsty. "Sea salt removes outer layers." They grind sea salt into their skin. "Twig tea cleanses intestines." As the hot liquid moves through them, they lie back, let their brains drain and become empty. My sister goes to the baths to transform herself. There are many legs here, some ugly, some lovely. The steam sauna is a beautiful and dangerous place. Mythological creatures stroll through the mist, transforming into old women with fat encircling their wrists, into young women with bones like jewelry. If only my sister were small enough that I could hold her in my palm. She'd sit cross-legged on my lifelines, telling jokes. The women instruct one another: "This is what you do with cucumbers." "This is how you plunge into the cold pool." "This is how you wash your innards." "This is where you rub peppermint oil so your thoughts get cool, placid." A confession: I'm terrified by something inside my sister's refrigerator. I've seen a bowl of flawless fruit decay until it became a gray apocalypse. If my sister were three inches tall I'd take her away. I wouldn't let her open that refrigerator ever again. In a large house as lovely as a dessert, my sister walks down the hallway, enters the kitchen. A metal bowl filled with beautiful plastic oranges. No spiderweb and no strand of hair would ever dare mar this house. She opens a glass door. Outside, two lounge chairs. Trees and sunlight all around her. My sister wears that same nervous, grinning expression she wore when she forgot her lines in the kindergarten play. What has happened to us? What has happened? I've heard rumors of a man who can cut houses cleanly in half with a chainsaw. Tomorrow, my sister will go to the baths.

drought #6

The last farmer in the world hears things to which we are deaf. Hears snowflakes hitting cow dung. Hears the moist, taut sound of chickens laying eggs. Hears the bones of small mammals snapping in the forest. Hears blades of grass slumping in drought. Hears his own innards going about their business. Hears his brain moving toward thoughts like a large, slow piece of machinery. Hears cells dividing in the womb of a horse, and hears the filly plopping into life some months later. Hears pollen hitting his eye and hears himself blinking.

He also hears his invisible wife rolling the piecrust, sprinkling flour, rolling the piecrust, sprinkling flour. Hears the joint between her femur and her pelvis popping when they do what they do at bedtime. Hears cells dividing in her womb, hears his invisible sons and daughters being put together bit by bit until they have lungs, eyelids, ears. When they sleep, he hears the noises made by the monsters in their dreams. When they go to school, he hears their brains learning numbers, a sound like many faucets dripping irregularly. At night, he lies awake, listening to his invisible family digest cornbread, butter, green beans, milk, bacon, blueberry pie. It is a symphony, and he grins. Someday he'll learn the word *symphony*.

As the farmhouse is demolished, certain items can be seen in the wreckage. A table. A chair. A cup. The windows splinter first, then the shingles, the walls, the floorboards. The kitchen goes, the living room, the mudroom. The upstairs bedrooms cave in. A mattress. A lampshade. A coffee can. A milk bottle. A pink slipper. A fork. You wonder why the farmer left these objects behind? You wonder why he is not here to watch it happen?

Already the last farmer in the world lives alone on the eighteenth floor of a skyscraper. The yellow taxicabs in the streets below bring to mind crickets. He wants to know how anyone can sleep what with the uproar of water and sewage moving through the pipes.

drought #7

used to be snow here, everything white and firm and ice; then mud came peeking through, and, mesmerized by the novelty, we surrounded it, exclaiming *So this must be spring!* for we'd only read about spring; aware of how humans are supposed to feel about spring, we waited eagerly for something green to appear, but instead the mud spread; we retreated to our homes, shamefully longing for snow; later, we noticed our floorboards becoming unstable beneath our feet, and rushing outside we saw that all the houses were sinking into the mud—but sinking very gradually, and our lives continue rather normally, with only minor inconveniences: we yank our mailboxes up from the mud every morning, trade our delicate snow-boots for mail-order galoshes, hurry after our babies whenever they sneak outside (we find them floundering and gurgling, delighted, sinking, mud wedged between their rolls of fat); meanwhile, the wrought-iron lampposts lining our streets (pet project of the Beautification Committee) become unmoored and crash down, their frosted glass globes shattering, leaving shards in the mud; the playground sinks quicker than anything, but the monkey bars remain, now only an inch high, and our resourceful children create games that involve hopping across the metal bars; the graveyard disappears; in the library the books are slimy with mud; and then comes one particularly discouraging moment: a Flexible Flyer sled, capable of making sleek sounds upon fresh snow, appears in a sinking public trashcan, its runners thick with mud, as dead as a sled can be; we try to go forth, we do!; leading their daughters down the aisle, wishing desperately to distract them from the mud on their lacy trains, fathers whisper *Seeing a bride is like seeing a unicorn*; grooms carry brides over reinforced thresholds, but even adding extra concrete to the foundation can't prevent the inevitable; still, newlyweds lie in bed and drink coffee and paint walls, pretending they're starting a stable life together. Eventually, though, it becomes impossible to ignore the fact that everything shall vanish, and we recall that there

the apocalypses

apocalypse #1

Now Tor has stormed out to go chop wood. We're fighting. An asteroid the size of seven houses is headed toward Earth. I discovered this yesterday, as did he. We are astronomers. We live at the top of a mountain in an undisclosed location. We have our telescopes, and our makeshift observatory. We enjoy the thinness of the air and the absolute quality of the silence.

When the asteroid arrives, the air surrounding it will become ten times hotter than the surface of the Sun. Wherever it hits, all life in a 150-mile radius will be obliterated. Light brighter than any light. Darkness moving thousands of miles per hour. Fires. Volcanoes. Tsunamis. A billion and a half people killed the first day. For many years, no sunlight will reach the surface of the earth.

I want to march down the mountain—when was the last time I descended? Five years ago? Twelve? Thirty?—and tell them. I'll tell their newspapers and magazines, their TVs and Internet. They ought to know they have nine days left. I like to think of them dancing in the streets, drinking $500 bottles of wine, making love, breaking the windows of stores, eating mangoes and caviar, staying up all night in the amusement parks, tossing rose petals down from roller coasters.

Tor prefers to imagine them going about their lovely mundane little lives, getting upset about foolish things and getting happy about even more foolish things. He thinks we ought to let them do whatever it is they do, fight and cry and fuck and be poor and be rich and irk out their nine final days until, much to their surprise, they die. Meanwhile, up here on the mountain, we will have slow sex late in the afternoon, and will feast on our store of dried chokecherries, and on the ninth day will lie out in the glen, waiting.

I cannot tell which of us is kinder. But here I am, filling the flask with water, tying the sheepskin around me, lacing up my boots.

apocalypse #2

All their lives they've heard the song: *She'll be comin'
round the mountain when she comes.* Sometimes it sounds
boisterous, sometimes mournful. Anyhow, they settle
at the foot of the mountain to wait for her. They bring
their chickens, their children, their rose-seeds. They
wait a long time. The chickens are slaughtered, and
the chickens' great-great-great-grandchickens. The
roses climb up and over fences. In the restaurant, the
man at table 14 sings *She'll be comin' round the mountain.* He has blessed many people by buying them
beer. *Who is she?* they ask him. He shuffles off to the
bathroom, his response lost beneath the music of his
urination. Things start to change—blue-breasted rob-
ins appear, people mistake fallen gloves for dead rats,
trails of sugar lead red ants into the courthouse—and
it seems that she'll be coming soon. Everyone goes
out to the meadow. They shade their eyes, look up at
the mountain. Entrepreneurs sell hotdogs, balloons,
sarsaparilla. Speculations fly left and right.

It'll be the Queen, holding the first potato from the New World in a lace handkerchief, one crisp bite taken, arrived here to begin a Potato Empire! It'll be a unicorn accompanied by six wild white horses, the unicorn saber-toothed and violent yet obedient to any command given by any child under the age of five! It'll be an invisible bride wearing a thirty-foot veil; when the young ladies reach for the fascinating fabric, they'll be transformed into a thirty-foot-long white dragon! It'll be someone named Mary! Anne! Helen! It'll be a humanoid seven feet tall, her body glowing like gold! It'll be a naked woman holding a gleaming apple! It'll be a girl as mild as spring but for the smell of scotch on her breath! It'll be an old woman in an enormous white hat! It'll be a fire, a blizzard, a tornado, a bomb!

The children get heatstroke. The roses get dusty. The Ferris wheel gets stuck. The man at table 14 leaves table 14. Weary, we sit down on the trampled field to wait.

apocalypse #3

When the subway fire begins, we keep our cool, as we've been trained. We don't remove our sunglasses. We don't take deep breaths in an attempt to figure out the source of the smoke. We stand on the subway platform, breathing shallowly, pretending we're merely smelling urine and old gum, chatting among ourselves, avoiding the topic of the fire that's raging somewhere nearby. We don't think about how many stairs stand between us and the outside. We don't entertain the possibility of claustrophobia. If there were a problem, the firemen would be here. If there were a problem, announcements would blare over the loudspeakers. There are no firemen and no announcements: ergo, we keep our cool. This is the logic in which the city has trained us. Disregard the smoke stinging your eyes, disregard the flicker of orange down the tunnel, disregard your claustrophobic heart. Don't sweat on your lovely fabrics.

But. What if one cannot control oneself? One rushes up the first flight of stairs, screaming, embarrassing oneself a thousand times over yet screaming, shrieking, and others join, following behind, letting their beautiful sandals fall off their feet, tearing their delicate garments, clawing at one another, up the second flight, the third, thousands moving upward, stampeding, sunglasses clattering to cement, up and up, arriving wild-eyed and sweaty on the street, panting in the glorious heat of the earth, trees, breeze, ice-cream truck—and then, shamefully, returning to the subway station, back into the intestines of the city, where the trains are running normally and no firemen have appeared, where the smell of smoke has dissipated and no flames can be seen.

Anticipating this trajectory, we stay right where we are, cool as cucumbers on the subway platform, wet-eyed and trembling behind our indifferent sunglasses, feeling a small sense of utter failure, not unlike the sense of failure felt upon using the air-conditioner for the first time each season, or upon seeing four turtles lining a concrete log in the city park, joyously stretching their silly chins up to the sun.

apocalypse #4

It's a terrible idea, yet we go ahead with it. We've seen disturbing signs: two chairs perched precariously on the edge of a city rooftop, as though someone is trying hard to recreate a home in a time when the idea of home is threatened. It seems that many catastrophic things are on the verge of happening. We're poor and have nothing, yet the possibility of the world falling apart disturbs us nearly as much as it disturbs the rich. Unlike them, we don't own a vehicle that could be used as a getaway car when chaos comes—but also unlike them, we're footloose, ferocious, ready to leave immediately, not moored anywhere by anything, not worried about precious objects of silver and whale-bone. We buy $15.00 wigs and drugstore sunglasses. We vaguely recall distant relatives who live in other, greener places. They dress countrified and are extremely generous. We met them once at someone's wedding; they were wearing corduroy! We pitied and admired their authenticity. Now we envision ourselves driving down the road to their farm. They're on the porch with lemonade. The bedroom they give us has a rag rug, a foggy mirror, a daisy. We milk cows.

Having served on grand juries, we know just how violent our city can be. We have fewer qualms than we used to about one brief crime, a few seconds of snarling aggression. Here, women get robbed on their doorsteps. Boys hide under beds in which their mothers are raped, in bedrooms from which their mother's jewels are stolen. People use bottles as weapons, and teeth. They fail to say "Excuse me." Truly it is time to leave. Our wigs sit lopsided on our heads. Our hands are bronze with blood. The discarded knife slices the oily river. Our hearts are resilient. They rise up with the twinkling birds of morning that dart over the highway. These birds seem to think they're already in the countryside.

The countryside—the countryside—the countryside consists of a concrete barn, a tiny trailer, a field filled with shit.

apocalypse #5

This is what happened: Your mother was sitting on the porch. It was August. The night of light. Everyone hung candles in silk globes on the gingerbread roofs of their cottages. Small kids ran around burning themselves with sparklers. Big kids shared one cigarette, an orange pinprick beyond the pond.

The cottages blazed from the inside too, lamps in living rooms illuminating gingersnaps glistening with sugar. Great-great-grandmothers' crystal bowls hosted radiant gumdrops. The punch glowed with its own pink light. A group of gay boys wandered among the cottages, singing sunny songs from a lighter era.

The oldest man in the world had been honored that night. They let him light the first candle, and then let him sit in the rocking chair where he sat for ten hours every day. He had things to tell people, yes he did, yessir, but the light had stolen his voice.

My darling, you who were not there, it wasn't difficult to be happy then. So much less difficult than usual. I found the darkest place, right beside the lilac bush, and lingered there to catch the last of the light before it got swallowed up by the thick fragrant black of the woods.

Your mother sat on the porch with two other old women. They all had red skin and flowerdy dresses. They looked as though they could answer any question in the world. I could think of a hundred I wanted to ask. But then the gay boys came by. More punch had to be made, and the seventh batch of gingersnaps pulled from the oven.

It was just then—as your mother held up the bowl of gumdrops for the gay boys, as the littlest kid discovered my hiding spot, as the older kids returned chewing gum—that lightning struck. Drawn by the many sources of light illuminating the cottages that night, it came down, trying to match our brightness with its brightness, it struck the roof of your mother's cottage, my darling, and everything everything everything began to burn.

apocalypse #6

Now that everything's on fire and there's no water anywhere, the violinist is the firemen's only hope. As he plays, his violin produces water. Using the smallest screws, they attach their hose to his instrument. Radiant orange flames stretch up fifteen feet, twenty. Tchaikovsky. Water starts to emerge from the hose. A drip. Then a stream, a torrent. The firemen attack the fire.

It's unclear to everyone whether the violinist is a guest or a prisoner. He's permitted to sleep four hours each night, in a protective concrete tomb in the graveyard. He's gotta sleep, the firemen agree. While he sleeps the fire gains ground. The firemen begin to feel hopeless. They wake him and give him a PowerBar— such a precious resource now, but remember how they used to inhale them during high-school football season? But hell. Who wants to remember. The smell of tackles ripping up a damp field. Grass and fog. Their sons will never know. There are no autumn football fields (woodsmoke, apples) in the skyscrapers to which families have retreated, claustrophobic but alive. Safe.

The firemen get angry, thinking these thoughts, and perhaps are somewhat rough leading the violinist back toward the fire. The fire is red and yellow and green and orange and blue and purple and white. Like bonfires in the woods after the games. Their future wives clinging to them. Look at those colors! the girls whispered, their skin hot and coppery.

The violinist has also been remembering. His parents, his friends, etc., the memories anyone would have. Nobody notices the slight slowing of his miraculous fingers. Violin lessons in a room that smelled of mothballs and raisins. Then, eventually, her. Hands hovering above piano keys. How dear she was. Sometimes crying for no reason. Sometimes flinging herself into his arms. Rolling dough into perfect spheres to make gingersnaps. Mournfully rubbing her uterus. Standing in the yard with a teacup as the fire approached. That's all.

The violinist drops his violin and walks away. Hey! the firemen shout. Come back! Stop! Hey! You!

apocalypse #7

The first sign of the impending apocalypse is that people start smoking cigarettes in the subway. Before, cops with gleaming badges would have materialized. But now? *Everyone* smokes, for we know our lives will be short no matter what. Subway cars fill with the delicate fog of cigarette smoke. It swirls overhead, makes us lightheaded, reminds us of those faraway days when cigarettes were legal in bars and smoke was a magic substance through which you could view dark, fascinating scenes—a woman leaning against a wall, drinking a golden liquid.

When the heart of the apocalypse beats right above us, we grab cartons of cigarettes and carry them underground. The subway is the final stronghold in the shattering city. We bring tuxedos and party dresses and booze and crystal and heirloom jewelry. When we get hungry, we eat things out of cans, but we don't get hungry much. We get drunk. We get smoky. There are, of course, moments of repulsion—issues concerning, for instance, the disposal of human waste.

But moreover: knowing we shall die, we're desperate for joy. We measure time by the number of dresses the women go through. "I've been partying for seven dresses," they report. We'll run out of cigarettes someday, yes, and booze, and even dresses, but our amassed resources are quite astonishing. The unreliable subway lights force us to rely on candles—how romantic we all look in the tremulous flame—but then sometimes the electricity flashes on, and we all cheer, drink deeply, throw glasses on the floor, divine tinkle of shattering crystal. Somebody turns up the battery-powered music and we're the best people in the world, carefree, mystically enshrouded in cigarette smoke, our voices rich as money. It's dark down here, and warm, like the nightclubs we always dreamed of.

When we emerge, old, pale, sick, the world is all tar and steam. We scream promises to the mustard sky: if we find one single blade of grass, we will redeem ourselves, we will change our life, we will change our life.

apocalypse #8

An extremely normal man walks past a park bench, a stoplight, a pigeon, a dog, etc. So certain is he of these objects that he can think about other things as he walks, which is why he fails to notice when the world becomes paper; he's agonizing about something in his briefcase.

Only as the snowflakes fall more thickly does he realize they're not snowflakes at all but rather scraps of paper. He looks up to locate the delinquents responsible for this prank . . . and finds that the trees are flat, two-dimensional, made of brown paper. The sky beyond has no depth. He sits on the park bench to relieve his trembling legs; it crumples beneath him, throwing him onto the stiff, papery grass. The pigeon takes flight, flapping its impossible paper wings. The stoplight changes: a circle of red paper miraculously replaced by a circle of green, as though large, powerful fingers switched them while he blinked. The dog is now a paper dog. As it runs toward him through the falling snow, its fur sounds like the pages of a book being flipped. This begs the question—and he looks down at his hands. They are indeed made of paper, carefully—even tenderly—cut into the proper shape. The dog sniffles kindly at his paper shoes.

The wind strengthens. It sucks up the grass. Piece by piece, it yanks the dog's paper fur off its body. Soon the dog is just half an ear, two legs, and a tail taped to a stick. The trees blow away. A panel of the sky blows away, leaving a rectangular gap beyond which emptiness can be seen. The man holds tight to himself. Another panel of the sky vanishes, revealing more emptiness. *Coming apart at the*, he thinks, but never completes the thought, for his arms are pulled off, his head, his—and soon all that remains of the entire world is a few pieces of wood, awkwardly nailed together to resemble the shape of the human body, floating in the universe.

the helens

helen #1

A young woman sits in a room, thinking of all the women named Helen Phillips who have ever existed. Many, many, many of them are dead. She would like to line them all up in a row. The young woman in the room is named Helen Phillips.

Someone once said to her: You ought to write more about people who are middle-aged, and also people who are old.

She recently discovered that the saddest obituaries are the obituaries of old women who lived long, happy, satisfying lives and are mourned by husbands, children, grandchildren, great-grandchildren. These are the obituaries that bring tears to the eyes of young wives. It does not make sense that these are the saddest obituaries; and yet.

The young woman leaves the room and walks out into a meadow of brilliantly green grass. Footpaths wind through this meadow, and in the middle of the meadow there is a white pavilion, and in the middle of this white pavilion there is a fountain, and this fountain makes the loveliest, quietest sound. There are many, many, many women walking around the meadow. All of these women wear large and fabulous hats in different shades of white. As Helen Phillips walks among the women, they slowly turn to her, and their faces are bright beneath their beautiful white hats, and their eyes aren't bloodshot. "I am Helen Phillips," each woman says before turning away again, and then adds, "I am 87" or "64" or "93" or "72" or "101," yet they all look as though they are twenty-five. Suddenly, Helen Phillips notices that she has a large and wonderful hat on her head; but she is not yet ready for such a hat.

A young woman sits in a room, thinking of all the women named Helen Phillips who have ever existed. She writes to them: Dear, dear Helen Phillipses, you who were once new to this world, you who once desired only milk and sleep: the world misses you, but only a tiny bit, a very tiny bit.

helen #2

You know that song "Lay Lady Lay"? Bob Dylan wrote that song about me.

There was no brass bed. It was just a mattress on the floor of someone's uncle's house. But we were young, and could easily imagine brass beds. I was eighteen. I was twenty-five. I was thirty-three. I was a sympathetic waitress. I was the loneliest girl in the high school. I was a belligerent offshoot of the British Royal family. I was a divorcée. I was a virgin. I was a baker. I was a laundress. I was a beekeeper. There was a place below my belly button and above my cunt where Bobby could rest his head whenever it all got to be too much for him.

"They boo," he said once. "They boo," he said a second time. "Boo," he said.

You can't even believe how skinny he was. It was like fucking a skeleton. Ashes from his infinite cigarette fell on my stomach. He was such a kid. I felt so bad for him.

He said, "What colors do you have in your mind?"
I said, "Wha?" He said, "Do you have any colors in
your mind?" I had no colors but I nodded. "Lemme
guess," he said. "Green?" "Sure," I said. "Gray?" "Sure,"
I said. "Ah fuck," he said.

I offered him the place below my belly button and
above my cunt, but he went to sit in the beat-up armchair. His clothes are dirty but his hands are clean,
Bobby sings. I don't think his clothes were particularly dirty, nor his hands particularly clean.

Did he ever call me by name? Was the armchair
maroon? Was it an armchair or a stool?

Bob Dylan, if you ever read this, if a published
page of writing may serve as my telegram to you, I
want you to know: My name is Helen. I grew up in
the foothills of Colorado. I believe I loved you as no
girl ever loved you. Every girl believes she loved you
as no girl ever loved you.

helen #3

Jack Kerouac and I are obsessed with making lists. He keeps track of the books he's read, and the women: name (nickname if he can't recall), dates, locations, number of copulations. I keep track of how many alcoholic beverages I drink each week, and how I feel each night, a smiley or frowny face beside the date. He and I wish to master the statistics.

But we're thwarted by the fact that we didn't start lists the instants we were born. I want to know how many times I've sneezed over the course of my life. I want to know how many scoops of ice cream I've consumed. I want to know exactly how many miles I've walked. One feels one's life slipping into obscurity. Jack Kerouac acknowledges that some women and some books have fallen between the cracks—I picture them falling between the cracks, the sidewalk splitting open, beautiful panicked girls clinging to the pavement while books plummet into the widening chasm.

If only there were someone who kept track of it all! I'm envisioning an infinite register that I could consult to find out how many words I've typed and how many I've deleted. Our desperate lists are so pitiful in comparison to the image of this splendid register. It's enough to make you throw up your hands. Jack Kerouac throws up his hands, standing by the window in the grayish light of a Brooklyn afternoon.

In Jack Kerouac's notebook of women, each page is divided into six boxes. In box #22, the name Helen P can be found alongside the names of five other women. Helen P? Helen P! Helen P, whoever she may be.

And now someone is two places at once. Standing here in a museum in the year 2008, staring at her name on a list. Lying there shivering under the sheet in the year 1951 while Jack Kerouac stares out at the naked February trees and the smoky Brooklyn sky, the image of two pale winter thighs and three orgasms already slipping his mind.

helen #4

In the factory where the virgins are made, we're given bread at noon. We eat it in the cement courtyard, sitting around the dry fountain, looking up at the broken windows. We are not ones to talk. We are virgins. This is the law, and a sensible law at that.

Our virgins are sent all over the world, to Guatemala, to South Africa, to France, to Cuba, to Brazil, to Poland, to Portugal. We mail them out naked. Father blesses the cardboard boxes. When they arrive at their destinations, they'll be dressed in the velvet robes that have been stripped off the outdated virgins. Our newer, better virgins—high-quality plastic, real human hair from our heads, eyelashes from our lids— will be placed in glass coffins that have been dusted for the occasion. I've wondered, but never asked, what becomes of the old virgins.

Instead, I've turned my attention to picturing how our virgins must glow against the great stones of cathedrals, and against the wooden walls in poorer countries. I've thought of their sad peaceful faces. I've always wondered why I am instructed to paint their lips with slight frowns. I've worked here for a decade, and it is an honor to be the woman who paints the lips. Still, certain things have been given up along the way.

Six months ago, when I first did it, I made it so imperceptible that Father would not notice, nor anyone else, until some girl in some church somewhere would pause before my virgin, would run down the aisle, would leave the building with a whoop, would feel finally, for the first time ever, blessed.

The complaints have begun to roll in. Father's displeased. The bishops cannot quite put their finger on what the issue is, but—something's amiss. Father has told us to work harder, to be more perfect, to not falter in making the virgins we've been making for decades. He says the troublemakers will be found, and punished.

When they come for me, I'll be ready, smiling an invisible smile.

helen #5

There's a woman in the zoo. We all go to see her. Her cage has brass bars. The back wall is painted amateurishly to resemble a forest. She stays very close to that wall, as though by pressing hard enough into it she may penetrate through to a real forest.

She shrieks whenever people are nearby, short swift shrieks, and pushes at the air to push us away, as though we're attacking her. Whenever someone sneaks an arm through the bars and skims a finger across her foot, she moans long and low and clings to the painted trees, shivering, pressing her forehead into the wall. She wears ragged bedroom slippers. The kindly zookeeper tells us that she screams if he tries to replace them with nicer slippers. She wears a white t-shirt and shapeless black sweatpants, worn through to gray in the buttocks. She's somewhat pretty, except that her eyes are bloodshot and she smells unclean. The zookeeper explains that he's powerless against her. We'd like to take her home and wash her; we picture ourselves gallantly leading her into a reasonable life. The zookeeper reminds us: *You can lead a horse to water.* . . .

It's said that her husband brought her in. One night when he touched her, she shrieked and hid in the closet. The next night, she hid under the bed. Suddenly, she couldn't stand the touch of any human. Couldn't ride the subway, couldn't go grocery shopping, couldn't share a bed. The poor young man brought her to the zoo, at a loss for what to do with a wife who had transformed from a human into something else. The plaque beneath the cage bears only her first name: *Helen.*

How weird, we say. Poor woman. Meanwhile, she shrieks. Heard from afar, these shrieks sound like the cries of the jungle birds in the zoo's jungle dome. Bizarre-o, we say. What a freak.

A confession: I have looked into her eyes while she shrieked, have seen there something not unfamiliar, have become envious.

helen #6

I am an extremely normal person. I live on the eighteenth floor of an impersonal apartment building; I work, I sleep. This is why it makes no sense.

The first morning it was simply an orange, there in the gray hallway outside my door. Such oversights do not typically occur in this carefully managed building; I was surprised, and delighted. What a splendid color it was! *It brightened my day*, I imagined myself telling someone dear to me. With the slight thrill of theft—dare I claim this as *mine?*—I put it in my bag.

The second morning: an elephant and two lit candles. Unlike the orange, *this* could not be misinterpreted; this was intended for me. The red rhinestone elephant looked dazzling as a whore in my beige living room. These were not items I wished to own. But if I left them outside, the conscientious janitors—

The third morning: four candles. Seventeen strewn marigold blossoms. A painting of a beautiful saint wearing purple. My apartment prickled with color. The fourth: eight candles, five oranges, twenty-nine marigold blossoms, three miniature brass body parts (eye, brain, uterus). . . .

And so it continued. Initially, I brought everything inside, transforming my apartment into a jewel-box. Yet soon I had no alternative but to let the altar—yes, that word came to me on the seventh day—flourish in the hallway. Oddly, the janitors do nothing about it. Soon it will consume this entire floor, and will have to move up to nineteen or down to seventeen. I can picture the day—not so far off—when all thirty-six floors are an altar.

I have seen them. They're lean, tired, nervous, and wear mended coats. Yet knowing they're near me, they stand up straighter. I'm not supposed to see them and vice versa; this is, clearly, the rule, since when they notice me peering out they tremble and flee, leaving marigolds and handwritten notes in their wake. These scraps of paper explain nothing: *Sunday the 10th* the script on one implores, or simply *Helen*, or *alegría*.

helen #7

Once a young man was sitting on a porch. Suddenly five girls carrying buckets of flowers appeared on the porch. They talked loudly to one another. Actually they weren't carrying buckets of flowers, but big old rusty blue coffee cans filled with flowers. The flowers were zinnias. These zinnias had been cut very recently. They still smelled like dirt. They were odd, brilliant colors. One of the girls was skinny with plump lips. Another was plump with radiant skin. Another was tall with small feet. Another had red hair and long fingers. Another had a long neck and gray eyes. Or perhaps one of the girls was skinny and long-fingered, perhaps one was plump and gray-eyed; the girls and the zinnias and the coffee cans merged and mingled and crisscrossed in his mind. The girls perched on the porch railing. Wherever they sat, the wood turned canary yellow. They began to sort the zinnias, tossing weak and wilting ones onto the floorboards, collecting the sturdiest blossoms. They ignored him. He watched them work. Eventually they gathered up their coffee cans and their chosen flowers. He knew they were going to leave. He would miss them desperately. "Where are you going?" he cried out. "Don't worry," they said, "we'll be back." "What are your names?" he said. "Helen," they replied. He watched them go; they moved like one enormous, perfect, prehistoric creature. The porch was no longer covered in canary yellow paint. The rejected blossoms had vanished.

Decades later, the young man was sitting on a porch. He was a very old man now. Five girls carrying coffee cans filled with zinnias appeared and surrounded him. "Hey," they said. "We're back." The porch painted itself canary yellow. They began to sort the flowers. They were subdued. They did not talk so loudly nor laugh so much. The floorboards became covered with shriveled and inadequate blossoms. The old man recognized the sensation of ecstasy. Eventually one of the girls addressed him. Her voice was solemn. "So, are you ready?" she said.

helen #8

Two old women walk very slowly down an institutional hallway. They are both named Helen. Helen slides her right foot less than a centimeter. Then Helen slides her right foot less than a centimeter. They move into a rectangle of sunlight. Later, they move out of it.

I should like to get past them. I have business to attend to. But they're impenetrable as a glacier. Helen is rather limp in the neck. She seems to be moving even more slowly than Helen.

"Don't worry," says Helen, her vocal chords creaking into motion like a wheelbarrow in March. "You'll get better."

"I will?" Helen croaks, her head sagging even deeper. A minute passes. They move forward fourteen inches. "When?"

"Hallo, Helen and Helen. Gettin yer exercise?" A pregnant, freckled nurse waddles swiftly down the hallway toward us. Her voice sounds weird and invasive. She spots me and winks. "Watch out, ladies, there's somebody behind ya." Helen tries to turn her neck to look at me but gives up, letting it droop downward onto her chest. "Now hang on just a sec, ladies," the nurse says, gently dragging their walkers to either side. "Thanks," I whisper, but something happens inside me as I pass through the twin gateposts created by Helen and her walker and Helen and her walker. Moving in slow motion, I turn around to look at them. The nurse has vanished. Glacially, Helen and Helen roll their walkers back into position.

"Who are you?" Helen says. "I'm Helen," I say. "Who are you?" Helen says. "I'm Helen," I say. "Who are you?" Helen says. "I'm Helen," I say. "Who are you?" Helen says.

They're old. They're hard of hearing. Forgive them. Walk away. Leave them behind.

Yet I should like to see them in white hats as big as swans. I should like to see them in a rose garden, turning their fragile necks beneath those enormous white hats. I want them to turn and look at me. They are lithe; the roses are heavy; it is noon.

helen #9

Glancing outside during the tea party, I notice dragons in the yard. "Excuse me," I say, "but why are there dragons in the yard?" The old ladies don't respond. They drink tea and wear enormous white hats. They're all named Helen. "Excuse me," I repeat, "but why are there dragons in the yard?" "There are no dragons," says one of the Helens. All of the Helens eat petit fours and sip from bone china teacups, blind, deaf, oblivious to the two bronze dragons lolling in the yard. The dragons aren't much bigger than horses, but their tails are long. Wisps of cigarette smoke emerge from their nostrils. They have amber eyes, as I observe when one of them looks directly, scornfully, at me—ashamed, I stop staring. Later, helping the Helens into their carriages—for they insist upon horse-drawn carriages just as they insist upon tea parties just as they insist upon being served by a modern young woman named Helen who cultivates old-fashioned mannerisms—I am surprised to hear a Helen speak: "Our world," she murmurs, "is a bone china teacup."

Later, returning to its high shelf a green glass vase that held now-wilted pink poppies during the tea party, I sense the world suddenly draining of color. Everything goes white, as though the vase placed just so is a key that has opened a door somewhere, a door from behind which colorlessness comes rushing out. I fall off the stepladder.

Later, searching for color, I discover a bush with tiny yellow flowers. Examined up close, the yellow petals are strange and stringy, hardly petals at all, but pickiness is no longer an option, and I allow myself a flash of happiness.

Later, a red bird flies past the window and vanishes.

Later, I look outside to check on the dragons. Instead of dragons, there are two horse-sized oil rigs in the yard. It's enough to make one doubt one's eyes. But which is stranger, unexplained dragons or unexplained oil rigs?

All of this is just to say: no world can last.

helen #10

Once there was a woman who lived with a man. She had many stories to tell; many odd and fabulous things happened to her. She was constantly sharing these anecdotes with him.

She'd begin, "When I was a kid I went to the park where our prehistoric ancestors can be seen" or "The old family farm in North Dakota is now underwater" or "My sister and I once posed for a Maxfield Parish painting" or "My father built a covered wagon" or "I walked to the North Pole" or "Whenever I swim in the ocean I hear whale heartbeats" or "I once served Noah honey mead" or "I know how to ripen a rotten peach" or "I had the Virgin Mary over for tea" or "There's an albino squirrel in the park" or "There's a woman named Helen in the zoo" or "I saw a monster in the forest" or "I saw a Neanderthal in the convenience store" or "Anne Frank tried to teach me how to fly." Surely she'd told him at least a hundred such anecdotes, if not more.

But then, at a party, when she'd say to some stranger, "I've seen Bob Dylan juggle apples," he'd link his arm through hers and say, "You never told *me* that." She'd stiffen with exasperation. "I've told you many times! Why do you never listen to a word I say?" Always, *always*, he reacted with surprise to selections from her stockpile of stories. It drove her crazy, made her feel incomplete, lonely, limping, robbed of any receptacle other than her own insufficient mind. "I want you to be my receptacle!" she'd exclaim, ignoring his grin. And yet they were happy, cobbling together enough tenderness to overcome the lack of listening. "My dear slug," she called him, and meant it.

When she dies somewhat before her time, he's able to recite every single anecdote she ever told him; all along he could have done it, and should have, but liked too much to hear her begin, again and again and again.

acknowledgements

I think of the letters that compose the syllables that compose your names: the A's! the B's! the C's! the D's! the E's! the F's! the G's! the H's! the I's! the J's! the K's! the L's! the M's! the N's! the O's! the P's! the Q's! the R's! the S's! the T's! the U's! the V's! the W's! the X's! the Y's! the Z's!

My agent, the steadfast Faye Bender. My editors, the courageous Lisa Graziano and Michael Graziano. The fairy godmother Rona Jaffe Foundation. L.S. Asekoff, Michael Cunningham, Jenny Offill, Elissa Schappell, Ellen Tremper, Mac Wellman, and the Ucross Foundation, for early encouragement. Julie Agoos, James Davis, Joshua Henkin, Janet Moser, and the phenomenal Sarah Brown, for day-in day-out everything. The brilliant members of the Imitative Fallacies: Adam Brown, David Ellis, Tom Grattan, Anne Ray, and Mohan Sikka, with special thanks to Marie-Helene Bertino, Elizabeth Logan Harris, and Amelia Kahaney. The good people of the Brooklyn College MFA program, especially Jeanie Gosline, Elliott Holt, Andy Hunter, Scott Lindenbaum, Joseph Rogers, and Margaret Zamos-Monteith. The delightful ladies of the Bookettes. All my lively students. Avni Bhatia, Cynthia Convey, Adam Farbiarz, David Gorin, Lucas Hanft, Audrey Manring, Jonas Oransky, Laura Perciasepe, Genevieve Randa, Maisie Tivnan, and Tess Wheelwright, for advice literary and otherwise. Gail and Doug Thompson, in-laws extraordinaire. Mary Jane Zimmermann and Paul Phillips Sr., *grand*parents. All my siblings: Katherine Phillips, Mark Phillips, Raven Adams, Peter Light, and Nathan Thompson, with infinite thanks to my sister Alice Light, astute reader and swift responder. My mother Susan Zimmermann, who taught me to be brave. My father Paul Phillips, enemy of sentimentality, friend of sentiment. Adam Thompson, two chairs, one bed.

Grateful acknowledgment is made to the publications where the following pieces first appeared, some in slightly different form:

American Fiction, Volume 11: The Best Previously Unpublished Short Stories by Emerging Authors (Flood #1, Flood #2, Flood #4, Flood #5, Failure #5, Failure #7, Far-Flung Family #6, Drought #1, Drought #2, Drought #3, Drought #4, Drought #5, Drought #6, Drought #7, Apocalypse #3, Apocalypse #5, Apocalypse #6, Apocalypse #7); *Brooklyn College Magazine* (Helen #4);

Electric Literature Outlet (Apocalypse #8);

Faultline (Flood #3, Fight #9, Bride #4, Wedding #3, Helen #1);

Hotel St. George online (Mistake #2, Monster #4);

The Hotel St. George Infinitely Expanding Library of New Fabulist Fiction (Fight #3, Wedding #2, Wedding #4, Wedding #6, Wife #7);

Opium Magazine online (Bride #1);

PEN America (We? #5, Fight #1, Fight #2, Bride #2, Bride #3, Wife #1, Wife #8, Punishment #4);

Salt Hill (Flood #6, Regime #1, Regime #2, Regime #3, Regime #4, Regime #5, Regime #6, Regime #7, Regime #8, Regime #9, Regime #10, Regime #11)

Small Spiral Notebook (Mother #1, Mother #2, Mother #4);

Sonora Review (Helen #8);

They Are Flying Planes (Envy #3).

the author

Helen Phillips is the recipient of a 2009 Rona Jaffe Foundation Writers' Award, the 2009 Meridian Editors' Prize, and the 2008 Italo Calvino Prize in Fabulist Fiction. Her work has appeared in the *Mississippi Review* and *PEN America*, among others, and in the anthologies *American Fiction: The Best Previously Unpublished Short Stories by Emerging Authors*. A graduate of Yale and the Brooklyn College MFA program, she teaches creative writing at Brooklyn College. Originally from Colorado, Phillips lives in Brooklyn with her husband, artist Adam Thompson. Visit her website at www.helencphillips.com.

About the Type

This book was set in Adobe Caslon, a typeface originally released by William Caslon in 1722. His types became popular throughout Europe and the American colonies, and printer Benjamin Franklin used hardly any other typeface. The first printings of the American Declaration of Independence and the Constitution were set in Caslon. For her Caslon revival for Adobe, designer Carol Twombly studied specimen pages printed by William Caslon between 1734 and 1770.

Designed by John Taylor-Convery
Composed at JTC Imagineering, Santa Maria,CA